MUTINY IN SPACE

MUTINY IN SPACE

ROD WALKER

CASTALIA HOUSE

Mutiny in Space

Rod Walker

Published by Castalia House
Tampere, Finland
www.castaliahouse.com

Editor: Vox Day

ISBN: 978-952-7065-61-7

Contents

and one of his Social colleagues set a bomb-trap to surprise the police. Unfortunately for Dad, his colleague botched the job, and accidentally blew up my father, himself, and the other members of their cell without killing a single cop.

In retrospect, I suppose my dad may not have been that smart after all.

Mom didn't seem to miss him too much, because one of my earliest memories is watching my mom's newest boyfriend working on our couch, swearing and chain-smoking while he wrote his thesis. Mom had a lot of boyfriends and I hated all of them. They were either University intellectuals, which meant they never shut up about how the hyperspace revolution and mankind's expansion into the Thousand Worlds had rendered capitalism and religion obsolete, or they were Party sympathizers, which meant they had lots of tattoos, smoked non-stop, and devoted themselves to their search for the eternal buzz, either electronic or pharmaceutical.

Come to think of it, I'm not all that fond of my mom, either.

So with my dad blown to bits by his idiot friends, I had two precisely male influences in my life that didn't either lecture or ignore me. One was my older brother Sergei. I thought the Social Party was stupid, but Sergei didn't. Maybe he wanted to impress my mom, or maybe he admired her Social Party boyfriends, or maybe he wanted to follow in my father's footsteps. He joined the Social Youth and became a teenaged Party radical, which for most kids would have been rebellion. In my family, that made him a momma's boy. Of course, being a card-carrying radical, he got into a lot of trouble, and I usually got into it with him, because, let's face it, raising Cain is a lot of fun if you're sufficiently young and stupid.

My other male influence was my uncle Corbin.

He grinned "Some of the guys at the meeting will know how to make fake IDs, and we can buy some liquor. If you want to meet hot girls, that's the way to do it."

I hesitated. I should have said no. I really, really should have said no.

"Sure, why not?" I said. "Let me get my coat."

And that's how we went to hear Alesander Ducarti, the greatest revolutionary of our time, speak.

Chapter 2

Revolution is the Bomb

The gathering was not far from the main spaceport of New Chicago, close to the Starways Hauling Company landing pads and hangars where I helped Corbin repair the company's freighters. Social Party diehards, various academics and administrators from the University, and younger guys like Sergei gathered to hear the speech at an abandoned warehouse. They only filled about half the space. The Social Party, despite repeated efforts, had never become anywhere nearly as popular on New Chicago as it wished.

So we had plenty of room to get close to the improvised stage, which meant I had a good, long look at Alesander Ducarti.

He was noticeably different from most of the other people in the warehouse. If you've met the typical Social on a world that the Party doesn't actually rule, you know what I mean. The men were mostly middle-aged and doughy, while the women were either skeletally thin and heavily tattooed or morbidly obese with dyed hair and various body modifications.

By contrast, Alesander Ducarti looked strong and fit, with thick black hair and deep black eyes over a nose like a hawk's beak. He reminded me of the mercenaries who sometimes came through the spaceport, hard men with harder eyes.

Corbin and the other techs always kept well clear of the mercs, and I had followed their example. Ducarti looked *dangerous*. I couldn't put my finger on it, but I didn't like him. I was, I realized, *afraid* of him.

At the spaceport, you could always tell which guys would be dangerous and which were just loudmouths blowing off steam. Ducarti looked like he could kill someone without even blinking.

Even before he opened his mouth, he held the crowd of Party members rapt, and it made me think of a herd of sheep staring at a wolf.

"Brothers and sisters of the revolution," said Ducarti. He had a deep, resonant voice, calm and controlled. "I must commend the great work you have done on New Chicago. Step by step, you have spread the message of the Social Party through this corrupt society. It is true that your brothers and sisters on other worlds have known more success. Other worlds now are governed by the just hand of the Party, their oppressors liquidated and their populations now know greater equality than ever before in their history. Other worlds have, to date, done more to bring the cause of universal revolution to mankind. Here, you have been hindered by the corrupt oppressors of New Chicago's government, and that is why you have been able to accomplish less. But the work you have done here, brothers and sisters of New Chicago, has been no less valuable to the revolution!"

They applauded. I looked around, bewildered. Why were they applauding him? Couldn't they see that he had just insulted all of them?

Ducarti's speech went on and on, longer than I would have imagined possible, and the attendees applauded dutifully at all the appropriate pauses. After he finished and stepped back to thunderous applause and enthusiastic cheers, a pair of local Party officials made some brief remarks. Ducarti stood there listening with a faint half-smile, and I wondered if anyone else could see the contempt on his face. After the speech, the crowd moved to the tables along the walls, where refreshments had been provided. I suppose the Party couldn't plan to overthrow the government without cheese and crackers.

"Sergei, let's get out of here," I said in a low voice. "You said we could go after the speech was done."

"In a minute," said Sergei, craning his neck around, looking for someone. "I just want to meet Ducarti first."

"Oh, there you two are," said a woman's voice.

I turned my head as Mom joined us, and I fought down the urge to laugh. She had done herself up for the occasion, complete with the requisite chain-bracelets. It was always funny to see how women dressed for Party meetings. The official Party doctrine rejected things like makeup and jewelry as tools of the oppressors, so Party women who wanted to make themselves look prettier tended to go with tank tops, tight jeans, and high-heeled boots, and wear chains and tools as decoration. Despite her age, Mom was still in good enough shape to pull off the look, though God knows some of the heavier women looked like too-much sausage squeezed into too-little casing.

It suddenly occurred to me that Mom wanted to make an impression on Ducarti, and my amusement turned to disapproval. I couldn't think of anything to say that wouldn't set her off, though, so I didn't say anything.

"Why, Nikolai, I'm surprised you're here," said Mom, delighted.

I gave an indifferent shrug.

She offered me a brittle smile and turned her attention to Sergei. "Sergei, I would like you to meet Alesander before he goes. He has excellent connections. He will be able to help you advance in the Party, whether you stay here or go off-planet."

"But Sergei," I said. "You said–"

"We'll go in a bit," said Sergei. "You heard what Mom said. Maybe he'll set me up with something good!"

Mom led us through the crowd, and soon we stood before the stage, where Ducarti was speaking with several of the local Party officials. He turned as we approached, and his dark eyes swept indifferently over us, finally setting upon my mom.

"Ah, Professor Rovio," said Ducarti, with an enigmatic smile. "So good to see you again. These are your sons, I take it?"

"Yes, Alesander," said Mom, beaming at him. "This is my oldest, Sergei, and my youngest Nikolai."

I shook hands with him. I didn't want to, but I didn't see how I could avoid it. His hand was cold and dry and hard, and strong enough that I suspected he had spent a lot of time lifting weights."

"You both remind me of your father," said Ducarti. "Did you know that I knew him? Fine man. A true believer in our cause. If he had been on the Central Committee of Novorossiya III instead of some of those other fools… well, suffice it to say, Novorossiya III would not have fallen again to the reactionaries. But we must dwell upon the future, not the past, for it is our revolution that offers the best hope for all humanity."

"It is indeed, Alesander," said Mom, her eyes all but sparkling as she looked at him. She really liked him, and

I suspected she intended to visit his hotel before he left the planet, her current boyfriend notwithstanding. My contempt for them all sharpened. Couldn't they see Alesander Ducarti for the con man that he was? Why were they all fawning over him as if he was a rock star or something?

"And you, Sergei," said Ducarti. "I understand you recently joined the Party."

"I did, sir," said Sergei. I blinked. Sergei never called anyone "sir." My big brother straightened his back and stuck out his chest as Ducarti looked at him. "I joined as soon as I turned eighteen. I want to serve the Party like my father."

"Excellent," said Ducarti, as a ghost of a smile crossed his lips. "With the help of bold young men like you, we cannot fail." The predatory black eyes turned towards me. "And how old are you, Nikolai?"

"Sixteen," I said.

"And will you join the Party when you come of age as well?"

I almost lied and said yes to avoid causing a scene, but the contempt I sensed in him hardened my resolve.

"No," I said, meeting his eyes squarely.

The temperature in the warehouse suddenly seemed drop several degrees. Mom stiffened, and Sergei scowled. Ducarti, though, only looked amused. One side of his mouth curved up, just a little, as he glanced around the room, then returned his attention to me.

"Well, some must learn their lessons before they are convinced," said Ducarti. "What do you intend to do, if you will not serve the Party?"

"I'm going to be a starship mechanic," I said.

Some of the Party members listening to us laughed.

"A starship mechanic?" said Ducarti, smiling. "A noble profession. We are the Party of the workers, after all."

"Working how?" I said. "Flying from planet to planet making speeches for a living?"

"Rhetoric defines reality, boy," said Ducarti, his eyes narrowing. "There is no objective truth, only how mankind perceives that truth. The task of the Party is to define the proper truth for mankind, the truth of the classless society we shall construct. Everything else is irrelevant."

"Isn't that just an educated way of saying that you make stuff up?"

Silence abruptly fell over the Party members close enough to hear the conversation.

"Nikolai," said Mom in warning, but Ducarti waved her quiet.

"We serve a higher, nobler purpose," said Ducarti. "We work to end all oppression and all inequality. One day, all humanity shall speak of the revolutionaries of the Social Party with the same reverence now wasted upon Christ and Buddha and Joseph Smith. There is nothing wrong with practical skills or fixing starships, Nikolai Rovio, but as a son of the Revolution, you have more potential than that. If you waste that potential by voluntarily embracing the chains of the oppressors, then you will sacrifice your chance to rewrite the course of history."

I was sick of his pompous words and his stupid accent, and his naked contempt made me want to punch him. I just wanted to leave. I had decided to go home by myself when Sergei spoke up.

"He is right! We are sons of the Revolution, not workers. You stain our father's memory by talking like that!"

"Father's memory?" I said, my temper snapping. "Hey, Ducarti, our dad got himself blown up, right? Someone screwed up a bomb." The spectators shifted nervously, and my mom turned white with anger. "Maybe if he had learned some of those practical skills, he would have known how to put a bomb together and not gotten blown himself up like some stupid…"

I didn't see it coming. Mom slapped me, hard. Harder than I would have expected. The blow snapped my head around and I lost my footing for a second.

"How dare you," she whispered. "How dare you do this to me, here of all places."

"Yeah, Mom," I said, glaring at her, wiping a drop of blood from my lip. "Because that's what is wrong here. You being embarrassed in front of the high and mighty Mr. Ducarti, the great revolutionary."

Ducarti looked genuinely amused for the first time that evening. "All shall be equal after the revolution." He looked at Sergei. "However, since it is clear that you, at least, are a true son of the Social Party, Sergei Rovio, I have a task for you."

"You do?" said Sergei, straightening up. "Really?"

Ducarti produced an envelope, an expensive-looking thing embossed with the official seal of the Social Party. "One of the Party's projects has been to circulate a petition demanding an increase in the estate tax to seventy-five percent. We now have adequate signatures to require a referendum. It should be one hundred percent, but sometimes it is better to eat the steak in small bites than to choke on the entire thing." He offered it formally to Sergei in both hands. "I want you, as the youngest member of the Social Party on New Chicago, to present this petition at the appropriate government office."

"Me?" said Sergei, his eyes widening. "That's… that's a really big honor, sir."

"Oh, it is," said Ducarti, still grinning. "It most certainly is. As the face of the Social youth, as a true son of the Revolution, I think you are the perfect man to deliver our message."

"I will go at once," said Sergei.

"Good man. Also, as our official representative and voice, I insist you take one of the Party's vans, emblazoned with the red hammer of the worker raised against the spiral of the galaxy. Think of what a sight it will make when the van pulls up, and every eye turns towards you, and you stride forth to present our petition to the corrupt, illegitimate authorities of New Chicago. We shall, of course, alert the media, so that the moment will be recorded."

"Absolutely," said Sergei proudly. "I'll do it."

"I'll go with you," said Mom. She smiled at Ducarti. "I would like to see my son take his first steps in service to the Revolution."

"As you wish, Professor. And you, Nikolai?" said Ducarti, the cold eyes turning back towards me. "Will you accompany your brother as he assumes his birthright among the men of the Social Party?"

"No," I said, stepping back. "I'm going home. I'll walk. I don't want to ride in a Party van."

"As you wish, boy," said Ducarti, still smiling, although it now struck me as more cruel than sardonic. "Go home. Go play with your engines. The Revolution does not require you yet."

A gale of laughter went up from the Party members, and even Mom and Sergei joined in with the others. That hurt more than I would have thought. I whirled around so they could not see my burning eyes and I stalked from the warehouse without another word.

My defiance, combined with Ducarti's contempt, saved my life.

I went home, but because I wasn't watching the news, I didn't see what happened. As soon as Sergei and Mom left in the van, Ducarti returned to his ship and immediately launched. From his ship safely in orbit, he monitored the progress of the van, watching until it reached the central planetary administration building fifteen miles from the spaceport.

Once the van reached the offices, in full view of the cameras that had been alerted, the fusion bomb hidden within the van was triggered.

Sergei and Mom were killed instantly, of course. The forensics techs finally found some of Sergei's teeth and a piece of Mom's femur, but nothing else. Five thousand, six hundred and ninety-two people were killed in the explosion and the resultant collapse of the nearby buildings, and over eighteen thousand were hurt or wounded. The minute the bomb went off, Ducarti left the system, escaping to hyperspace before the system defense ships could close in on him. But before he hyperjumped away, he sent out a broadcast announcing that the bomb was an act of revolutionary justice against the planetary government and people of New Chicago for failing to embrace the principles of Sociality.

The reaction was as swift as it was violent.

The next day, the planetary government of New Chicago by an executive order of the emergency commission outlawed the Social Party. A lot of people were arrested over the next month, including most of the non-science faculty of the University. Pretty much every official in the local Social Party leadership was executed without trial as a co-conspirator, whether they had actually known about it or not, and a lot of other people were charged with various crimes.

As for me… I really didn't get into too much trouble over it. I spent four days in the offices of New Chicago's Internal Security Division, not far from the smoldering wreckage of the building my brother and mom had unintentionally destroyed, while a dozen different interrogators asked me the same questions over and over again, looking for any inconsistencies in my answers. I was too shell-shocked to try to lie or defend myself, but it didn't matter. A dozen different people had been recording Ducarti's speech, including my confrontation with him at the end, and it was patently obvious that I had known nothing about his plot.

Of course, neither Sergei nor Mom had known the truth, but both the media and the government officially claimed that they had been in on the plot, and that they had knowingly sacrificed themselves for the Party and for the Revolution.

But to this day, I don't think they knew the truth.

What I sometimes wonder is if it was my fault that Ducarti chose them. If I hadn't just said yes when he asked me if I would join them, would he have chosen some other patsy to drive the van? Would he have chosen Sergei anyway? Or maybe he would have even asked me to drive it. But every time I start blaming myself, I remind myself that I wanted to leave. I even tried to leave, but Sergei insisted on meeting Ducarti.

If anyone is to blame besides Ducarti, it's Sergei. That's what I tell myself, anyhow.

Chapter 3

Everybody Hates His First Boss

I was still a legal minor, so when the executions stopped and the dust finally settled, Corbin wound up with my legal guardianship for the next two years. We went to the funeral of Sergei and my mom together, and we were the only ones there. All of Mom's friends had been executed, arrested, or were keeping a low profile, and none of them could afford to be seen at the funeral of the man and the woman most of the planet blamed for the atrocity.

None of the life insurance policies paid out, so with what was left of Mom's savings I bought a small plot in the middle of nowhere, and that's where we buried their pathetic remains.

Corbin and I stood alone at the grave.

"You thought about what you're going to do next?" said Corbin.

I shrugged, staring at the cheap little marker stone. "Not really. There's not much money left. I've got enough for about three months' rent on the apartment, and that's all of Mom's money. I don't think I'll be able to get a job, and there is no way I can go to the university now."

"No," said Corbin. "Even before this, your family did not have a very good reputation with the authorities." He shrugged. "You know I tried to warn Sergei. And your mother. I really tried. But they simply would not listen. They could not see Sociality for what it really is. They were seduced by the vision. Your father–"

"What about my father?"

Corbin met my eyes. "He was my brother and I loved him, but Nikko, he was not a good man. He might have been a good man once, but the Party transformed him. In the end… I am afraid that he was very much like Alesander Ducarti. Forgive me for speaking ill of the dead, but that is truly what happened. Your mom was a long way down that path, and your brother had just begun upon it. If they keep you from it, their deaths may have been as a blessing."

I wanted to get angry at him, but I couldn't.

"It's not speaking ill of the dead," I said, "if it's the truth."

"I suppose not," said Corbin. "Listen, Nikolai. I'm not your father, and I might be your guardian for the next two years, but I don't have the right to tell you what to do. By the time I was your age, I had already fled Novorossiya III to get away from the secret police there. Now I've got a new berth with Starways, a senior mechanic slot on a long-range freighter. What that means is that I can choose my own apprentices. The company prefers to hire experienced men, but it doesn't mind training up new ones so long as someone sufficiently experienced is in charge."

I blinked. "Are you asking me to join you at Starways?"

"I am," said Corbin.

"Won't they be pissed that everyone in my family was a terrorist?" I said. "Except you, of course."

Corbin shrugged. "New Chicago isn't all that big of a place. It's a backwater, really. All the Thousand Worlds are out there, Nikolai, and New Chicago is just one of them. Even if you don't want to stay with Starways, you can put in some time, find someplace new to live once you get your feet under you."

I thought about it for a moment, but there really wasn't anything to consider.

"All right," I said. "One condition, though."

"What's that?" said Corbin, frowning.

"We never come back to New Chicago again."

Corbin looked relieved. "Deal."

That afternoon we drove to the local Starways office, and I signed all the necessary papers. The next morning, I spent the remainder of Mom's money on the tools I would need and gathered together everything I wanted to keep in a pair of footlockers.

Three days after that, Corbin and I left New Chicago on board the *Rusalka*, a long-distance freighter, and I began my new life.

My first year with Starways and the *Rusalka* was uneventful, but it was busy, busy, busy.

Let me tell you about my first love, the *Rusalka*. She was a big, ugly ship, and she looked like a fat gray trash can with an sublight engine bolted to the end, but she was old and tough and she was good at what she did. She could move five hundred thousand tons, so Starways used her for the heaviest jobs, such as moving comet ice to colonies, or transporting an entire wheat crop, or hauling immense quantities of ore from asteroid belts and heavy metal planets. She was a true starship, so she couldn't put down in an atmosphere, which meant cargo shuttles had to carry her loads down to planetary surfaces in relays. She could dock easily enough with orbital stations or deep-space platforms, though.

Keeping her spacing was a lot of work. And a big chunk of that work fell upon Corbin and me.

The *Rusalka* was nearly a kilometer long, but for such a massive ship, she didn't carry much crew. The crew compliment was only one hundred and thirty, and Corbin's official rank was Master Technician. Beneath him he had a dozen technicians and one overwhelmed apprentice.

Each technician had a different area of expertise and focus—life support, ion thrusters, mechanical systems, cargo handling robotics, weaponry, gravitics, and so forth—but we all worked together as a team on the bigger jobs, both for the sake of efficiency and for cross-training in case of accident and illness. I spent a lot of time with Corbin, but he regularly rotated me out to each of the specialized techs to learn their systems. Starways Hauling Company did not hire from any of the major universities, since so many of them were infested by Social Party members and their curricula reduced most of their graduates to uselessness, so the company maintained its own certification program.

That was to my advantage, because once I finished four years of apprenticeship, I could take the tests and get my own technician's certificate without ever having to set foot on a university campus.

I liked life aboard the *Rusalka*. The work was hard, but it was never boring, and I learned something new every day. Alas, there wasn't much opportunity for mischief. Nothing could kill a man faster than the hard vacuum of space, and if a crew member slacked off during a hyperdrive overhaul or an airlock refitting, his carelessness could doom everyone on board the ship. That awareness of constant danger hung over everything we did, and the crew knew it had to work together to survive.

Mom used to say nothing united people quite like a common enemy, and aboard the *Rusalka* we all had a common foe—the airless vacuum, the hard radiation, the possibility of hyperspace navigation errors, space debris, and a thousand other hazards.

To summarize, everything in space wanted to kill us, and we were always aware of that.

We spent a lot of time in space because the *Rusalka* took unusually long trips, and we would spend three or four weeks in transit at a time. Everyone called human-inhabited space the Thousand Worlds, but only something like one to five percent of stars had planets capable of supporting human life. So human-inhabited space really ought to have been called the Hundred Thousand Worlds, but I suppose that was too much of a mouthful. To get from one colony planet to another, the *Rusalka* had to hyperjump through ten or twenty or even thirty barren systems first, like a kid jumping over a stream using stepping stones.

However, just because a system was barren didn't mean it was uninhabited. Sometimes enterprising merchants set up refueling platforms, or the sort of space stations where they offered goods and services that were illegal on most of the Thousand Worlds. Miners dug out rare ore from asteroids, and a few enterprising colonists carved out tunnels on barren moons and built elaborate hydroponic setups. There were a lot of little colonies out there like that, usually founded by religious fundamentalists or political extremists of one kind or another.

There were also a lot of dead little colonies like that, because, as I mentioned, space is dangerous.

In addition to the natural hazards, pirates also liked to set up shop in deserted systems, along with slave traders based on one of the Prophet worlds. Sometimes the pirates worked for themselves, sometimes they were government-sponsored privateers, and sometimes they were Social Party revolutionaries.

So in addition to maintenance and repair, we spent a lot of time in weapon and self-defense drills. I discovered that I wasn't a very good shot in real life despite my years of experience playing shooters. It was a bit of a letdown, to be honest.

Corbin had a lot of friends among the crew. He had been with Starways for a long time and served on a bunch of different ships. Our executive officer was a man named Robert Hawkins, and he looked the part of the dashing captain from a movie. Apparently he and Corbin had served together in the Coalition navy before joining Starways, and Hawkins took it upon himself to teach me how play poker. The ship's computer operator was another old friend of Corbin's, a man named John Murdock. He was taciturn, sullen, and ill-tempered, but very good at his job. Whenever I needed something from him, he produced it with no more complaint than a sour glare.

The youngest technician on the ship had been Corbin's previous apprentice, and he was named Arthur Rodriguez. He was in charge of cargo robotics, and he was close enough to my own age that we became friends. We spent a lot of time playing video games in our off hours in the technicians' lounge. I won the racing games, but he always won the first-person shooters. Our favorite game was *Gunno-Tatakai*, probably because we each tended to wind about half of the time.

Overall, I liked working on the *Rusalka*, and I got along with most of the crew. They were nothing like my mom's friends, which I appreciated. I don't know what Corbin had told them before I came aboard, but none of them ever said a single word about the bombing or my family.

There was only one fly in the ointment… but it was a pretty big fly.

We all hated the captain.

Captain Thomas Williams looked the part of a sober starliner captain—tall, a bit paunchy, with a magisterial gray beard and a dignified bearing. If he was in a movie, you would expect him to stand stoically upon the bridge while the ship went down and the women and children headed for the escape pods. The first day I met him, I expected him to stop and make a speech.

Instead he scowled at me and glared at Corbin.

"What's this?" said Williams. "He looks like you, Mr. Rovio. You hook up with a stripper on New Chicago seventeen years ago?"

I blinked a few times.

"No such luck, sir," said Corbin. "This is my nephew, Nikolai. I've taken him on as a technical apprentice."

"Did you, now?" rumbled Williams. He squinted at me. "You'd better listen to your uncle, boy, and work hard. You look like a hooligan. Are you a hooligan?"

I was half-impressed by the perceptive observation. I had, after all, indulged in my fair share of hooliganism on New Chicago.

"No, sir!" I said, then amended my statement in the interest of honesty. "Never on board this ship, sir."

"Good! I'll have no hooligans on this ship, Mr. Rovio." He flicked a finger against my forehead, marched off, and as near as I could tell later, entirely forgot about my existence.

So Captain Williams was a jerk. That wasn't so bad in itself. A man can be a jerk, and so long as he's competent, in space it doesn't matter so much. The problem was that Williams was both incompetent and lazy. He spent days inside his cabin, refusing to emerge for any reason, and Mr. Hawkins served as de facto captain on those days. Frankly, Hawkins would have made for a better captain anyhow. Whenever Williams finally emerged from his cabin, he made a mess of things. He interfered with work schedules, or gave orders that added several days to our delivery times without any discernible reason, and sometimes did things that made no rational sense.

The crew worked around him as best they could. I was a new kid, "green as vat-grown algae" as Murdock liked to say, but even I could see that Williams didn't know what he was doing. To the experienced crewmen, he must have been intolerable.

"Why does he still have a job?" I asked Corbin one day as I helped him rebuild an oxygen scrubber on the crew deck.

Corbin grunted and held out a hand, and I passed him the appropriate size of wrench. He blinked at it and looked at me.

"How did you know to give me the five-eighths wrench?" he said.

"Because," I said, "you're removing the oxidation module. That means the five-eighths."

"Good," he said with approval, loosening the bolts. "You're learning."

"I can only learn by asking questions, right?"

"Right," said Corbin.

I glanced around the corridor, but the crew deck was deserted at the moment.

"So why does a guy like Williams have a ship and you don't?" I said.

"Because he's the captain," said Corbin.

"He might be the captain," I said, "but even if he used both hands, he couldn't find his own…"

"Nikolai," Corbin cut me off and I shut up. "It's against company regulations to criticize the captain."

"To his face," I said. "In public. Anyhow, I'm not criticizing, I'm asking."

Corbin sighed. "Very well. If you must know, nepotism. His brother is on the company's board. His younger brother, I should point out. I suspect Thomas Williams has always been the family's–"

"Black sheep?" I suggested. Corbin passed me the five-eighths wrench, and I handed him a screwdriver.

"No, they haven't cast him out," said Corbin. "Their incompetent sheep, let us say. He's bounced around from one career to another without making a mark, and he finally had to beg his brother for a job. Of course, the relative of a board member can't do something useful like repair work or navigation, no, of course not. He has to be a bloody captain, so the rest of us just have to deal with him."

"That's not fair," I said.

"World's not fair," said Corbin, checking the air filter in the scrubber.

"We're not on any world right now," I said.

Corbin snorted, unimpressed. "Universe isn't fair, then. We've both learned that the hard way."

"True," I agreed. "So what do we do when an idiot is the captain?"

"Stay out of his way, mostly," said Corbin. "We do our jobs and we get paid. It's Mr. Hawkins's job to deal with the captain, which is why he makes the big money. Such as it is. That's why I buy Hawkins a bottle of brandy when we complete our runs. He deserves it. Besides, I doubt the captain will be with the *Rusalka* much longer. Sooner or later he'll get rotated to another ship. Meanwhile, we'll just do our jobs and let Hawkins handle the captain."

That was sensible advice.

However, I soon discovered that neither Corbin nor Hawkins were actually following it. One day Corbin left a file open on his device while he was checking an airlock, and I saw that he, Hawkins, and Murdock had been recording a list of the captain's various misdeeds and derelictions of duty, complete with date, time, and ample supporting documentation. Sooner or later, I realized, they were arranging to get Thomas Williams fired.

I was fine with that. Especially after the incident on the bridge.

It happened about three months after I joined the *Rusalka*. A bridge console had blown some fuses, and replacing them was a time-consuming and tedious job, but a simple and necessary one nonetheless, which made it a perfect job to fob off on a technician apprentice.

I gathered up my toolbox and the replacement fuses and drove a little electric cart down the main dorsal corridor to the bridge. The *Rusalka* was a big ship, and all the vital areas were scattered around the gray metal cylinder of the cargo hold, for redundancy in case of asteroids or radiation or attack or space debris. Walking everywhere was much-needed exercise, but sometimes you needed to get places in a hurry, and that's where the carts came in handy. Plus, that toolbox got heavy fast.

The steel blast doors hissed open, and I stepped onto the bridge, which was mounted on the front of the ship's dorsal ridge. It was a big oval-shaped room with consoles lining the walls, windows of transparent armor-alloy looking into space. That day, we were making our way through an empty system to the next hyperjump point, and a sullen red giant blazed off the ship's port side like a big, cranky eye. Mr. Hawkins sat at the executive officer's console, and a half-dozen other crewers sat at their stations.

I hesitated a little when I saw Captain Williams in his chair, but he took no notice of me. He was, in fact, playing a card game on his device. That violated all kinds of rules, and I imagined Hawkins had already made a note of it in his file.

"Rovio," said Hawkins, turning in his seat. "The younger."

"Sir," I said. "Corbin sent me for the cargo console."

"Yeah, you had better do it now," said Hawkins, gesturing at a console in the corner of the bridge, its displays dark. "If we have to coordinate the drones from the cargo bay, it will double our unloading time."

"That long, sir?" I said.

"Maybe even longer," said Hawkins. "Trying to unload a ship with each drone doing its own thing takes forever. Time is money in this business."

"Yes," said Williams. Both Hawkins and I glanced at him. The captain hadn't looked up from his game. "Then stop jawing and get back to work, both of you."

I felt an overwhelming urge to ask him about his card game, but I managed to restrain myself.

"Yes, sir," said Hawkins. "Rovio, you heard the captain. Replace those fuses."

"Sir," I said. I crossed to the console, pushed the seat out of the way, and got to work. For some reason, whether from stupidity or malevolence, or possibly both, on the part of the designers, the fuses in the console were located behind the backup power supply and the local hard drives. So to swap out the fuses, I had to disconnect the power supply, pull it out, unmount the drives, and put them aside. Then I would have to install the fuses, boot the whole thing up, and do an integrity check on the drives and the console's processor.

I had removed the power supply and was just starting on the first of the three hard drives when a boot clanked against the deck.

I looked up to see Captain Williams glaring down at me.

"Captain?" I said.

"A question for you," said Williams.

I saw Hawkins watching us from his station.

"Should I finish the console first, Captain?" Pieces of it were scattered on the deck around me.

"It can wait," said Williams. "There is something I want to know."

"Yes, sir," I said, waiting for the question.

He stared at me, scowling, and I realized that he wanted me to stand up. My uncle had taught me never to leave my tools scattered around a job and he had also taught me never to walk away from an unfinished job unless my bladder was about to explode or I was spraying arterial blood or something, and that training screamed for me to pack up my tools and get the wires out of the way.

But I already been told it could wait, so I got to my feet instead.

Williams strode to the far end of the bridge, where the windows looked out upon the *Rusalka's* scarred hull and the blackness of space beyond. For the most part, the kinetic deflectors kept meteors and other debris from carving up the hull, but here and there I saw scorch marks where something had gotten through them. Beyond, I saw the sullen fire of the red giant star, and the blaze of the star fields. We were far enough out that the sun's light didn't drown out the stars, and it was a magnificent sight.

You can't get a view like that planetside. Unless the planet has no atmosphere, in which case you are choking to death and do not have time to contemplate the view.

I glanced at Captain Williams, and saw that he was frowning. "Well, Mr. Rovio," he said in an unfriendly manner.

That couldn't be good.

"Yes, sir," I said.

"What do you think of the *Rusalka* so far?" said Williams. "You've been aboard for what, two months now?"

"Three months, sir," I said. "And she's a fine ship, Captain, with a good crew."

Williams nodded. "Corbin Rovio speaks very highly of you."

"Thank you, sir," I said.

"But he is your uncle, you know. Of course he would speak highly of you."

I'd been warned about this. The Captain's moods were as volatile and as unpredictable as a solar storm. He could turn from friendly and joking to coldly furious on a dime, often for no discernible reason. I would wonder later if he was mentally ill.

It would explain a lot of what happened.

"I… am glad I have Mr. Rovio's confidence, Captain," I said. "I can't say as to his reasons for it, sir, but I hope it is because my work has been satisfactory."

Williams waved a hand. "The other crewmen have spoken well of you so far. I read the reports, you know. I'm the captain of this ship, and I have access to everything on her." His cold and inexplicable anger sharpened further. "I could have you thrown off the ship. Order you off at our next stop. Your uncle couldn't do anything to stop me."

Had I somehow done something to anger the captain? I couldn't imagine what it might have been. This had been the longest conversation I'd ever had with the man. I wanted to run, or at least ask what I had done to anger him so, but I suspected that showing weakness in front of such an unpredictable man would be a terrible mistake.

"Has my work been unsatisfactory, Captain?" I said at last.

"A ship's captain does not concern himself with such minutiae," said Williams loftily. "Though I will say neither Corbin nor any of the others have complained about you. You may recall I said that I wanted to ask you a question."

I nodded, still unsure of where he was going. "Yes, sir."

"I understand your family was heavily involved with the Social Party on New Chicago," said Williams.

Fear flooded through me. I wasn't anyone important, to the ship or to the Party, and the captain had already made it clear he did not care about me. Yet Hawkins and Corbin and Murdock had that file full of Williams's malfeasance, and perhaps the captain had become suspicious of them.

"I'm not a member of the Social Party," I said. "Neither is my uncle. The police confirmed that."

"What? I don't care about that," said Williams. "When you were on New Chicago, the day before your brother blew up that building…"

"He was tricked!"

Williams made a dismissive gesture. "Yes, he was innocent, I'm sure. I don't care. You met him in person. What was he like?"

"My brother?" I said. I felt like an idiot, staring at the captain, but the man's moods and questions shifted so fast I had trouble following. For a moment I didn't know what to say. What could possibly I tell him about Sergei?

"Your brother?" said Williams with a scowl. "Why would I care about him? You met Ducarti. What was he like?"

I blinked again. "Ducarti?"

"Yes, Alesander Ducarti," said Williams. "The Social who was behind the attack. You met him in person. You talked to him. I know you did—I saw the video. What was he like?"

"He was a liar," I said.

"Okay, what else. What was he like?"

"Um," was all I could come up with at first, as I wished that someone would call him and get me out of this strange interrogation. "He could give a speech. He was really good. I saw him give a speech to the Party members there and they ate it up. He was like a politician, but a smooth one. Except there was something hard about him. Like a soldier or something. He was… scary."

Williams grunted again. I had the sense that my answer hadn't pleased him.

"Why do you want to know, Captain?" I said.

"That will be all, technician apprentice," said Williams. "You may return to your work."

"Yes, sir," I said.

Williams had dismissed me, but for some reason he strode off the bridge and went through the blast doors to the main dorsal corridor. I stared after him, blinking and quite thoroughly confused.

"What was that about?" said Hawkins, getting out of his chair and joining me.

"I don't know, sir," I said. "Really, I don't."

Hawkins let out a displeased noise and glared at the blast doors. "He must be in one of his moods."

I was about to suggest that Hawkins and Corbin add the incident to their file of Williams's various misdeeds, but I decided not to. They wouldn't like that I knew about it. Besides, asking bizarre questions of an apprentice wasn't grounds for firing. But it was strange.

"Mr. Hawkins," I said. "Can I ask you a question?"

"Sure," said Hawkins, still looking irritated. "You can ask me anything you want, but you might not get an answer."

"What is wrong with the captain?" I said.

Hawkins shrugged. "I have no idea." He lowered his voice. "Don't repeat this, but if I had to guess, I'd say he's the family screw-up. He only has this job because of his brother, and he hates his brother. So he takes it out on the rest of us." He shrugged again. "It could be worse. At least he's lazy. That makes it easy to work around him. God knows there's nothing worse than a hard-working incompetent."

"Yes, sir," I said. "Hopefully I'm the first but not the second."

Hawkins blinked, and then laughed. "Finish up that console, Mr. Rovio, and then we'll see."

"Yes, sir," I said, returning to my tools and the half-disassembled console.

After dealing with whatever lunacy was dancing around inside the captain's head, replacing the fuses in a cargo console seemed like a nice day at the park by comparison.

After my shift was over, I went to the technicians' lounge and wound up playing *Gunno-Tatakai* with Arthur Rodriguez. Thankfully he had the music on mute. Whoever had programmed the game had been fond of ancient music, and the game's soundtrack was a nasty cacophony of flutes and drums that sounded like the inept efforts of an overly earnest reenactment band. It didn't save its sound settings either, so the awful music always blasted at top volume every time it started so you had to remember to mute it before you launched.

Fun game, though, if you're into that sort of thing. The campaigns took time, but there wasn't much to do on the ship if you weren't working.

"He's a weird one," said Arthur, gripping his controller and scowling at the display on the wall as his horseman trampled his way through a row of infantry, banners waving. "The captain, I mean."

"Yeah," I said, sending my archers to terrorize Arthur's spearmen. "Why do you think he wants to know about Ducarti?"

Arthur shrugged, which made his whole frame twitch. He looked like a tall, brown-skinned scarecrow, and the only time he ever stopped twitching was when playing games or repairing robots. "Dunno, man. Maybe he's just weird. Some guys collect pictures of serial killers and war crimes, you know. Maybe he's into that."

"Maybe," I said, dubious. "But I don't think so. He wasn't geeking out about the guy."

"Or he could be a deviant," said Arthur. "Like he has a bunch of dead babes in his cabin. Or he has a thing for terrorists."

"I just hope he's not a revolutionary," I said.

"The captain a Social?" said Arthur, mashing at the buttons on his controller as his horsemen trampled some crossbowmen. "Nah, his family is rich."

"Why else would he want to talk about Ducarti?"

"He doesn't seem like the type to join the Socials," said Arthur. "Back home, they were always freaks, you know? They were either ugly women who dyed their hair blue or the kind of men who take classes at the university for twenty years. And they were all kind of obsessed with blood and mayhem, although they never actually did anything about it like Ducarti did."

"You just killed, like, a hundred infantrymen," I pointed out.

"That's different," said Arthur with solemn dignity as he slaughtered my crossbowmen. What *Gunno-Tatakai* lacked in music, it more than made up for in lovingly rendered gore. "Besides, the Socials actually believe their own nonsense. The captain doesn't seem like he believes in anything but sleeping through his shift."

"True," I said. "If the captain was with the Socials, I bet we could get him fired. No one, not even his family, would trust an interstellar freighter to a Party member."

"I wouldn't," said Arthur, "but I just fix robots."

We turned our full attention to the important matter of crushing the enemy army.

After that unsettling encounter on the bridge, Captain Williams ignored me. I was fine with that. Life aboard the *Rusalka* settled into a routine, and I kept shadowing Corbin and the other technicians, learning everything I could. Six months after I came aboard, I was able to pass the first-tier certification, which meant I got a raise—which was nice even if it was a small one—and my uncle started trusting me with more important work.

Then, a year and a half after I started, the *Rusalka* received a contract for a very big job.

There was a new colony out in a system named New Sibersk, founded by refugees who had fled Novorossiya III during the collapse of the revolution there. That meant the colony was just about as old as I was. After seventeen years of grinding away at farms and infrastructure, the colony had finally produced a huge crop of wheat, and they were now seeking to bring their enormous surplus to market. The colony's legislature put out a call for bids, and Starways won it, mostly because the *Rusalka* was one of the few freighters big enough to take the entire crop in one trip.

And also because it was such a long trip. New Sibersk was on the outer fringe of the Thousand Worlds, so far out that the system hadn't even been charted until a few decades ago.

"Fifty-two hyperjumps?" I said, standing with Corbin as he looked at the mission manifest on the display screen in the technician's lounge. "Are you kidding me? That will take forever!"

"Actually, we'll be starting from the depot here," said Corbin, tapping one of the systems, "so it'll be fifty-nine hyperjumps in all."

"Man," I said, doing the transit times in my head. "That means a round trip of, what, two and a half months?"

"You'll have time to finish the next certification tier," said Corbin.

"And then some," I said. "That is a lot of uninhabited systems."

"Not all of them have been charted properly, either. We'll probably pick up some additional revenue running full scans and selling them to the Coalition navy when we get back."

I frowned. "Is that legal?"

"So long as the scans are accurate, yes," said Corbin. "If they're not accurate, then it's fraud. Or you could get charged with deliberately wrecking ships. That's an old trick of pirates. Sell screwed-up navigational charts, wait for ships to blunder into the wrong gravity well, then show up and steal their cargoes."

"Seems like some of those empty systems would be a perfect hiding place for pirates," I said.

"Oh, yes," said Corbin. "Or religious fanatics, or undocumented scientists working on unethical experiments in secret, or crazies trying to build the perfect society with an asteroid mine and a hydroponics bay. I'd guess that we'll pass by two or three dozen off-the-books colonies, mines, and space stations."

"And pirates," I said. "Don't forget the pirates."

Corbin remained unruffled. "We'll only see them if they're stupid. That's why she has all those guns."

The *Rusalka* did have a lot of guns. She was a big ship, which meant she had a big fusion reactor to power her sub-light drive and a big hypermatter reactor to catalyze the hyperdrive. Those reactors met she could generate a lot of power, enough for a dozen railgun turrets as well as the radiant and kinetic deflectors. She was well-crewed too, since Security Chief Nelson continued to insist that the crew drill every week with the weapons, and the man regarding missing a weapons-and-boarders drill as something worse than blasphemy.

"Or if they're really smart," I said.

Corbin shrugged. "Speak softly and carry a big stick. We don't go looking for trouble, but if anyone comes looking for it, we'll give them enough to choke on."

So the *Rusalka* left the company depot on the edge of the Thousand Worlds and began the long trip to New Sibersk. It took us just over the expected six weeks to get there. You'd think the crew would go stir-crazy during a trip that long, but God knows that Corbin and Hawkins kept us too busy to cause any trouble.

For one, there was all the endless maintenance. Corbin made good money as a master technician, and the reason he did was that the *Rusalka's* systems were locked in a never-ending war against entropy, and entropy never, ever, gave up. Simple routine maintenance filled up most of my days, interrupted by major projects when something broke or needed refitting. Studying for certifications took up most of the rest of my time, and when I had the occasional hour to relax, Arthur and I would connect to the ship's computer, grab some controllers, and either blow away aliens or fight a quick battle in *Gunno-Tatakai*.

The only downside? No girls. None whatsoever. Some companies hired female crew, but Starways wasn't one of them. I noticed that whenever the *Rusalka* came into a port, most of the unmarried men (and a few of the married ones) rapidly disappeared into various discreet-looking buildings with red lights over the front doors.

That was something I planned to investigate in more detail when I turned eighteen in a few weeks and could accompany the others. Arthur and I had tried twice to delve deeper into the mystery, but after successfully sneaking off the ship, were turned away at the door both times. When Corbin heard about our excursions, he scared us both to death with stories about what might have been our fate if we'd chosen the wrong sort of red-lit building to visit. We decided we were happy with our current employment and remained onboard after that.

We reached New Sibersk without incident. The colonists had three old AstroSpace HT-9 cargo shuttles. Between all three shuttles and Arthur's cargo drones, we managed to get the entirely of the wheat crop loaded in three and a half days. Arthur worked around the clock for those three days, and I helped him manage the robotic arms and drone systems that unloaded the cargo containers of wheat and secured them in the *Rusalka's* cavernous cargo bays. I learned a lot about automatic cargo handling during those four days, along with more than I ever really wanted to know about robot programming.

Turns out programming the cargo robots properly is really, really important, otherwise they start putting containers in the wrong places and the whole thing becomes a hideous and ruinously expensive mess. Fortunately, Arthur, Corbin, and the other techs knew what they were doing, and we got the ship loaded with no major incidents and only two or three equipment breakdowns.

We left New Sibersk and headed back towards the Thousand Worlds, and life settled back into the previous routine, though we saw even less of Captain Williams. Hawkins had more or less become the de facto captain by this point, which was fine with everyone. I kept working, and studying, and I thought I would soon be ready to take the next certification test. Then I could become a junior technician in my own right.

We were on our twenty-fifth hyperjump home when we found ourselves with unexpected company.

The empty system didn't have a name, just a designation—NR8965. Likely some astronomer's bored research assistant had slapped the designation on a list a thousand years ago, and it had stuck ever since. It was a binary star system—NR8965A was a red giant—and NR8695B was a smaller, hotter blue star paired with it. I thought the combination made them look like the galaxy's biggest pair of Christmas lights. The system had nineteen planets—twelve rocky, airless inner ones, and seven gas giants, each with their own moon system—three asteroid belts, an Oort cloud, and the usual Kuiper belt. A bunch of the rocky planets had valuable mineral deposits, but no one had gotten around to mining them, at least not officially, most likely because the radiation from the blue star drove up the overhead costs. A few of the gas giants had moons in the habitable zone, so a colony would likely wind up here someday.

I was working with Arthur that day. We had a day and a half of sublight transit until we reached our next hyperjump point, and Corbin had decided to use that time to fix a longstanding network error between the automated cargo robotics and the central computer. Arthur blamed the problem on the central computer's process handling, while Murdock blamed it on Arthur's programming. They had both complained to Corbin about it at length, and in exasperation he finally ordered them to lock themselves in the computer room and not come out until they had figured out what was going on.

And, lucky me, it was my day to shadow Arthur.

So at 0600 I staggered into the computer room, still trying to wake up. It was a small room located midway along the dorsal corridor, with one wall covered entirely with sixteen screens showing various computer functions—running processes, storage usage, CPU utilization, network balancing, and so forth. Arthur was already there, tapping away at a console.

As for Murdock, think of what a typical computer programmer looks like, then imagine the opposite. He looked like a middle-aged weightlifter who had just started going to fat, but was still capable of cracking some heads if he got irritated.

At the moment, he looked *very* irritated.

"The problem," he said, "is your programming logic. It has too many subroutines and dependent loops. Too much information comes through, and the interface–"

"No," said Arthur. "The problem is your outmoded network interface." Murdock's eyes narrowed, but Arthur didn't back down. "It doesn't have enough capacity. It can only process sixteen sets of instructions at a time. That's like taking a fire hose and trying to spray it through a straw."

Murdock folded his arms. "If your programming logic wasn't so inefficient, it wouldn't clog my interface."

Arthur scoffed. "There are thirty-six different cargo drones all running at the same time. Every single one of them has an independent programming set. Of course a lot of data is going to go through the interface. What, you want to run less than half of them at a time? We'd still be loading up at New Sibersk."

"You," said Murdock, pointing at me. "You've been quiet. What do you think?"

I hesitated. Actually, I thought they were both right. Arthur's programming did tend towards the heavy side, covering contingencies that hardly ever happened. That said, Murdock had locked down access to the main computer to the point that the drones had trouble communicating with it.

I opened my mouth to point that out, when an alarm I had never heard before went off.

It was the call to general quarters.

Arthur was the first to check the main. It seemed someone on the bridge had sighted a ship, and given that the system we were in was supposed to be uninhabited, the assumption was that it must be hostile.

"I can't stay here," said Arthur. "I'm on the damage control team for the cargo bays."

Murdock grunted, waving him off with one hand while he reached over to set a flip a row of switches below the monitors. "Then you'd better get going, hadn't you?"

Arthur vanished out the door. Murdock started typing commands, and then glanced up at me.

"Why are you still here?" he said.

"Well, I don't actually have an assignment for general quarters."

His scowl deepened. "Really? Suppose no one got around to it. Well, you can make yourself useful. You know how to do a CPU usage trace?"

I nodded.

"Sit there," he pointed at one of the chairs below the screen of monitors, "bring up a combined CPU, network, and cooling trace on five, and tell me if it does anything weird. Got it?"

"I got it," I said, sitting down. I took a moment to orient myself with the controls, typed a sequence of commands, and brought up the usage display. It was one of the basic principles of cyberwarfare. In battle, ships often tried to hack each other's systems with various forms of malware attacks. The ideal hack, of course, was one that went unnoticed by both the ship's defensive software and the ship's computer operator. Some things were impossible to conceal, however, and one of them was the heat generated from increased activity in the ship's processors... such as the increased activity from a malware process might produce. So the ship had a system dedicated solely to tracking CPU and network usage, and any anomalous activity got flagged.

Murdock busied himself by switching the computer systems to battle mode. That meant blocking any outside transmissions, switching priority over to the battle systems, and activating automatic defensive programs. Once that was done, he entered another command, and the sounds of the bridge came over the room's speakers, and I heard Hawkins giving orders.

Murdock must have seen my look of surprise. "One of the advantages of running the system. You know about things before everyone else." He pressed a button. "Let's see what we've got here."

The sensor display came up on another screen. Two ships were approaching the *Rusalka*. One was a blockade runner, small, fast, and heavily armed and armored. The other was larger and slower, and looked like a troop transport. Details filled up the display as someone on the bridge ordered a sensor focus of the blockade runner.

It was a dangerous little ship, and capable of menacing most freighters, but it was no match for *Rusalka*. Once the kinetic and radiant shields were up and full power sent to the defensive turrets, she would win any fight with such a small predator. The blockade runner could dance around the *Rusalka* for a few minutes, but the big freighter could shrug off the blockade runner's guns, and it would only take a single hit from one of the defensive turrets to cripple or destroy the runner.

That troop ship, though, presented a more serious threat.

"What are they thinking?" muttered Murdock.

The troop ship wasn't a big one. That class of ship could hold maybe forty well-armed soldiers, and didn't have any weapons except a laser cutter mounted to the prow, permitting it to slice through both the inner and the outer hulls of a ship However, the *Rusalka's* radiant shield would block the laser cutter, and the kinetic shield would keep the troop ship from ever making the contact with the hull required for boarding.

"Pirates?" I said.

"Mmm. Probably," said Murdock. His scowl deepened. "Dumb ones. They don't have nearly the firepower for something like us. So I wonder if they've got something else up their sleeves."

"Could they have… you know, like cloaked ships or something?" I said.

Murdock didn't come right out and say I was an idiot, but his expression said it for him. "I don't know what kind of crap shows they have on Nowhereville IX or whatever podunk planet you're from, but there's no such thing as a cloaking device." He waved a hand to encompass the entirety of the *Rusalka*. "This is a giant metal tube with reactors that could level a small continent if they go critical. Hard to make something like that invisible, isn't it? No, if they're going to go for an ambush, they'll have ships hidden behind an asteroid or a comet near our jump point, or something fast sitting behind one of the gas giants where we can't see it."

He snapped his fingers and pointed. "Hit that switch, and then that one, and run the macro that comes up on the display. We can listen in."

I reached over to the panel and followed his directions. A macro entitled "COMM/DUMP MAIN DRIVE" appeared, and I executed it. A sudden hiss filled the computer room, and for one alarmed moment I wondered if I had accidentally turned off the life support or something. Then I realized the speakers in the ceiling were back on, and a few moments later, Mr. Hawkins's voice filled the room.

"Unidentified vessels," said Hawkins, his voice cold and formal. "This is Starways Hauling Company freighter *Rusalka*, registry CIF-87334B. Request identification and statement of purpose. Repeat, request identification and statement of purpose."

The blockade runner and the troop transport did not respond, although both ships continued their approach.

"Unidentified vessels," said Hawkins, and lines of red text scrolled across one of the displays as the targeting computers went through their calculations. "This is Starways Hauling Company freighter *Rusalka*, registry CIF-87334B. Request identification and statement of purpose." His neutral voice took on a hard edge. "Be advised that our ship's defenses are now tracking your movements and we will respond to any hostile actions."

A spike appeared on one of the displays.

"Ah," said Murdock. "That got their attention. They're answering." He tapped a key. "Let's see what our bogeys have to say for themselves." A new voice crackled over the speaker.

I shot to my feet, my heart pounding, and both hands clenched into fists.

That voice! I knew that voice, deep and confident with the exotic accent I was sure was feigned. I sometimes had nightmares in which I heard it, followed by blood and fire and explosions.

"No," I shouted in alarm. "No! I know who that is."

"Freighter *Rusalka*," said Alesander Ducarti, Social Party operative, murderer, and interstellar terrorist, "this is the warship *Vanguard*, representing the legitimate government of Novorossiya III."

"Acknowledged, *Vanguard*," said Hawkins, his voice calm, even dry, "Starways Hauling Company does not take a position on local planetary wars. Also, system NR8965 is not claimed by any government, and whatever entity you represent has no legal authority here."

"Murdock," I said as I grabbed his arm. "You've got to call Hawkins. Now! Tell him to fire on those ships down, right now!"

Murdock frowned. "Why? They're acting like jerks, but we can't shoot first!"

"We have to! You know how I ended up with Starways, right?"

Murdock grunted. "Something about it."

"That's him! That's Ducarti!" I shouted, pointing at the *Vanguard* on the sensor display. "He killed thousands of people on New Chicago." My heart hammered in my ears as I jabbed at the screen. It felt as if the whole ship was collapsing in on me. "If he's coming after us, you can bet he has a plan. You've got to warn Hawkins. You've got to warn him right now. Right now! You've got–"

"Simmer down, kid," said Murdock sharply, but he was already typing. He wouldn't interrupt Hawkins's conversation with Ducarti, but he could send the XO a message. A moment later the screen flashed an acknowledgment from Hawkins, but I couldn't see what it was even though I stretched my neck out trying to read it.

"*Rusalka*, I must demand the immediate surrender of your cargo and ship," said Ducarti. "Alternatively, you may simply jettison your cargo into space and depart the system at once. Should you choose the latter, I will give you ten minutes to comply."

"Captain Ducarti," said Hawkins. "According to our records, just under two years ago you were involved in a serious terrorist incident on New Chicago that resulted in thousands of civilian deaths. Consequently you are a criminal and an outlaw. You have no authority over anyone, much less this ship."

"On the contrary, XO Hawkins," said Ducarti. "I represent the legitimate government of Novorossiya III."

"I imagine, Captain Ducarti," said Hawkins, "that the people of Novorossiya III have something of a different opinion on the matter. I also understand that the Social Party has been outlawed there."

"The people of Novorossiya III," said Ducarti in his smooth voice, "have fallen prey to reactionary propaganda, alas." I could easily picture his superior expression, and I desperately wished he was here so I could punch him in his stupid smirking face. "They shall be educated in time. Meanwhile, your cargo is the grain surplus of New Sibersk, and New Sibersk was settled by criminals exiled by the legitimate government of Novorossiya III. Consequently, as a representative of the legitimate Social Party government of Novorossiya III, I declare this cargo forfeit. I urge you, Mr. Hawkins, to jettison your cargo and continue on your way. It is the safe and responsible course."

My fists tightened at the self-satisfied purr in his voice.

"I am sure you have not failed to notice that our firepower is superior to yours, Captain. Like you, I would prefer that no lives be lost today. If you continue on your course, I am afraid we will have no choice but to defend ourselves, and lives shall indeed be lost… but most of them will be on the *Vanguard*."

"Indeed," said Ducarti, that self-satisfaction in his voice increasing. "In that case, Executive Officer Hawkins, I would like to speak to your captain."

"I'm afraid that Captain Williams is indisposed at the moment," said Hawkins.

"Are you entirely sure?" said Ducarti. "Perhaps you would like to double-check."

For a moment no one spoke.

Then Murdock started to swear, punching at keys as he did.

"We're idiots. Absolute idiots! I should have shot the wretch when I had the chance. Or dumped him out the airlock." His fingers flew over the keys. "We should have done something."

"I don't understand," I said. Murdock's uncharacteristic alarm was scaring me.

"I'm quite sure," said Hawkins. "This is your final warning, Captain Ducarti. Break off your attack vector, or we shall open—"

The speaker suddenly went silent. At exactly the same time, all the displays in the computer room went dead.

Murdock swore again, even more viciously, and yanked a metal box out from beneath the console.

The speaker came back to life, and a new voice came from the ceiling.

"*Vanguard*, this is Captain Thomas Williams of *Rusalka*," said the captain.

"What happened?" I said.

"He locked us out," said Murdock, opening the box. "The bastard locked us out. The captain has override codes to the entire ship." He flipped open the box, and my eyes got wide. There were four burst laser pistols in the box, along with extra power packs. "We should have listened to Corbin. He knew all along, but we didn't believe. More fool us."

"What do you mean?" I said.

Murdock opened his mouth to answer, and the captain's voice came from the speaker one last time.

"In the name of the Social Party and the Revolution, I hereby surrender this vessel, and order the crew to await instructions from Captain Ducarti."

Chapter 4

How To Handle Crew Disputes

For a moment sheer panic froze me where I stood. I had never thought to see Ducarti again. Now he was about to take control of the *Rusalka*. He would remember me, that I knew for a certainty, and he likely had a squad of Social commandos aboard that troop transport. He would shoot me the first chance he got.

Actually, he would shoot a lot more people than just me.

"We can't surrender," I said, the words tumbling out of me. I was badly frightened and trying not to show it, which meant I wound up talking real fast. "If we surrender, he'll kill us all. He's Social Party. He killed five thousand people on New Chicago. He'll kill everyone on the ship!"

"Rovio," said Murdock, doing something with one of the laser pistols. "Shut up!"

"Will the XO surrender?" I said. "We have to warn everyone." I crossed to the console and hit the phone switch, but it was dead. The entire console was dead. I pulled my phone from my belt, but the display only read SYSTEM LOCKED: COMMAND OVERRIDE.

"Rovio," said Murdock again, putting down the pistol and picking up a second one.

"That troop transport will land at the port airlock, probably," I said. "Maybe if we block it we can keep them from landing."

"Rovio!" bellowed Murdock. "Stop babbling and listen to me!"

I came to a stammering halt, blinking.

"Of course we can't surrender, you idiot," said Murdock. "They'll kill us all." He checked something on the last laser pistol and nodded to himself. "They're a Social strike force. When they take a ship, they kill the crew and make propaganda videos out of it. That bastard Williams! If he hadn't turned traitor, we could have blown the *Vanguard* to atoms. I knew we should've listened to Corbin."

"He knew?" I said. "You knew?"

"He knew. We suspected," said Murdock, shoving one of the pistols into his belt and taking the other in his right hand. "Corbin was sure of it, but Nelson and Hawkins and I weren't so certain. We knew he was an idiot, but a Social sympathizer? That seemed impossible. But we started watching him."

"That file you kept," I blurted out. "You thought he might be a sympathizer, so you were collecting evidence!"

Murdock gave me a flat look. "You knew about that?"

I shrugged. "I found out by accident. I didn't tell anyone. I didn't know what it was for. I thought you were just trying to get him fired."

"For a start," said Murdock. "If it turned out he was a Social, we would have gotten him sent to prison. Guess we figured it out a little too late."

"What are we going to do?" I said. I was so frightened I could feel tears threatening to spill from my eyes.

Murdock handed me one of the laser pistols. "You know how to use one of these?"

I hesitated, staring at the pistol's grip. I had never actually fired a gun at anyone. Granted, I had fired a gun plenty of times, thanks to Nelson's endless safety drills. More than once, I had grumbled about it, and Arthur and I had made fun of the dour Security Chief quite often.

Now, I was very glad he'd made me do it.

"Yeah," I said, taking the pistol and checking the power pack. The weapon was fully charged, which on a short-burst pistol like this one, meant about thirty shots. "Yeah, I do."

"Good," said Murdock. He gestured at the blank displays. "The captain has command codes that override everything on the ship. He's locked the system down, which means we're sitting ducks for Ducarti and his thugs. So I'm going to manually power down the computer, and lock it before it loads the operating system. That way I can take control of at least some systems and keep Williams from getting his fingers into anything."

"Can you do it from here?" I said.

"Nope," said Murdock with a grimace. "The idiots who designed this ship gave the computer its own power generator."

"Isn't that a good thing?" I said.

"Most of the time," said Murdock, "but the generator's all the way on the other end of the ship."

I grimaced. "That's not far from the bridge." We both knew that meant it would also be close to the most likely entry point for Ducarti's troops.

"You see the problem," said Murdock. He handed me a second pistol, so I turned the safety on the first one he'd given me and stuck it into my belt. "Let's move."

I nodded, gripped the pistol in the way Nelson taught me, and followed him out the door.

We stepped into the ship's main dorsal corridor. I didn't see anyone, but that wasn't surprising. The *Rusalka* was a huge freighter, and the crew was usually scattered the ship at their stations or on the crew deck. The main lighting had been turned off, and the emergency lights glowed in their rounded metal cages, throwing stark shadows over the metal walls and floor.

"He turned off the lights, too?" I said. At least Williams had left the gravitics on. He probably didn't want to have to maneuver his fat backside in zero-G.

"Zip it," snapped Murdock under his breath.

I started to defend myself, then realized that I was being an idiot, and shut up. My mind flashed back to the various instances of petty vandalism I had perpetrated with Sergei on New Chicago. He'd often told me to shut up on those little adventures too. Suddenly I found myself missing my older brother with a pain that felt almost physical… and a spasm of rage followed the grief.

If I got the chance, I vowed then and there, I was going to shoot Alesander Ducarti right in his haughty, sneering face.

Another part of my mind, the more efficient part, observed that wallowing in grief or rage right now was an excellent way to get killed, and that I'd better keep my wits about me if I, or any of the crew, was going to live through this mess.

So I zipped it and followed Murdock as silently as I could as we hurried down the corridor. For a computer operator, he seemed to know what he was doing. I'm not an expert on this kind of thing, but he was pretty quiet for a big man, the muzzle of his burst pistol swinging back and forth as he covered the corners. I suppose he had been in the Coalition navy with Corbin, so the navy would have trained him how to handle guns and move around a hostile ship. The *Rusalka* had a bunch of little battery powered carts for technicians to move around in a hurry when necessary, but they were tied into the ship's network, and Williams had locked those out as well. It was probably just as well. Sitting in those stupid little carts, we would have been sitting ducks for any Social commandos with halfway-decent aim.

The doors to the bridge finally came into sight. The bridge was sealed off by a pair of massive, reinforced blast doors, and both of them were closed and locked, the control panel shining red. The purpose of the doors was to seal off the bridge from intruders, and I wondered if Hawkins had managed to trigger them before it was too late. On the other hand, it was also possible that Captain Williams had locked the bridge crew in to keep them out of the way while Ducarti's men boarded the ship.

Closer to us, on the port side of the corridor, was the door to the emergency generator room. The generator for the computer system would be in there. On the starboard side of the corridor, closer to us, was an external airlock. The lights on the airlock's control panel were flashing, turning from red to green and back again.

That meant the airlock was cycling.

"Murdock," I hissed, pointing at the airlock.

Murdock stopped, scowled at me, and then looked at the airlock.

"They're already here," he muttered.

"They'll come through there, won't they?" I said, wondering if the two of us were going to try to hold them off with our pistols. I didn't like our odds. Apparently, neither did Murdock.

"I thought they'd cut their way through the hull," said Murdock. "But if the captain's letting them in, no need to bother." He shot a quick look around the corridor. "We can't stop them. This way! Go!"

I started to say that we could make the generator room at a sprint, and then a hiss came from the airlock, accompanied by the groan of laboring hydraulics.

Someone was opening the airlock from the other side.

I followed Murdock as he ducked into the nearest door on the port side of the dorsal corridor. We ran into a large rectangular room with a long table hosting a pair of computer consoles, and high windows of transparent metal offering a splendid view of the stars. It was the upper observation lounge. In theory, if the navigation computer was destroyed, the navigator could work out our position from the stars. In practice, the senior officers used the room as sort of a club house. Corbin had been in here a few times, but I never had.

"What are we going to do?" I said, looking around for cover and failing to find anything. We could hide under the table, I supposed, which would keep Ducarti's men from finding us for maybe three seconds. "There's nowhere to go from here."

"I know that," snapped Murdock. "Just close the door and lock it, now!"

That seemed like a good idea, so I hurried to the door and hit the release. It slid shut, and I locked it. The door had a small window at eye level, and as I stepped back, I caught a glimpse of the first of Ducarti's soldiers.

Ducarti might not have had many men aboard that troop transport, but what his commandos lacked in numbers, they made up for in sheer amount of armaments. The men I saw wore black body armor, layers of ceramic polished to a high sheen to refract and diffuse laser blasts and blunt the impact of kinetic firearms. They had black helmets with visors and air filters, making them look like humanoid insects. I wasn't an expert on guns, but I knew enough to recognize the kind of rifles the commandos carried: Tanith-Mordecai K7 full-automatics, with long 120-round magazines. They also carried pistols and grenades and things that looked like shaped charges.

We had clearly done the right thing by running. We wouldn't have lasted five seconds in a firefight with them.

I slipped away from the window. I knew Hawkins and the bridge crew wouldn't be able to put up a fight either. The crew generally didn't carry sidearms. I think Hawkins might have had one, but one gun or burst laser pistol was going to be useless against the kind of weapons the invaders were carrying.

"Murdock," I said.

"Yeah, I know, we're screwed," he said. He knelt next to the wall, working on something with his multitool. "They'll find us here unless we move. Which is what we're going to do, right now."

"How," I started to say, and then Murdock wrenched at the wall. An access panel popped away, revealing one of the narrow maintenance walkways that threaded its way between the inner and outer hulls of the *Rusalka*.

"Get in," said Murdock.

"That doesn't go to the generator room," I said, hurrying across the lounge.

"It gets us out of here," said Murdock. "And that's good enough for now. We can take the access tunnel under the corridor and come up on the other side, get to the generator room that way. Get in!"

He stepped back the access panel, and indicated that I should climb inside. I took a deep breath and squeezed into the narrow maintenance walkway. The floor was metal grillwork, thick coils of wire winding underneath us. Ducts and pipes and more wires hung in racks along the walls, though technically the wall on my right was the inner hull and the wall on my left was the outer hull. It was odd to think that only a meter or so of armored metal separated me from the vacuum on my right, though the inner hull didn't add all that much thickness.

"Move over," said Murdock as he followed me inside. He pulled the panel back into place, but since the mounting bolts were on the outside, there was no way he could secure it. He had pocketed the bolts, but the panel wouldn't stand up to a close investigation. For that matter, if the Socials had the right kind of sensors in their helmets and masks, they would be able to detect us moving between the hulls.

Murdock straightened up with a grunt, and I pressed against the wall again to let him move past me and take the lead. I followed him along the narrow walkway, the dim LED lights throwing tangled shadows against the wires and pipes and ductwork.

"Just a little further," Murdock muttered. A few yards ahead a cylinder opened in the wall on my left, revealing an access ladder that descended to the next level of maintenance walkways. He gripped the first rung on the ladder and started to swing himself into the shaft.

I grabbed his shoulder. "Wait," I hissed.

Murdock glared at me, then heard the footsteps below.

He swung back onto the walkway, and just in time, too. The ladder descended five meters to the next deck, which if I remembered right housed the senior crew quarters. About a half second after Murdock got clear, I saw the black-armored form of a Social Party commando stroll past, his K7 cradled in his arms and his finger on the trigger. Another half-second more and he would have seen Murdock. It would have been all-too-easy for him to spray the high-velocity, rubber-coated projectiles the Tanith-Mordecai fired up the ladder.

"How did he get in there so fast?" whispered Murdock. He rubbed his jaw with his free hand, thinking hard. "Wait. That means some of them must've gone to the crew quarters at once. Some of them are probably rounding up the crew and herding them into the galley, or somewhere big enough to hold everyone. That would make it easier to kill them all. Just seal the compartment, turn off the air, and wait for everyone to asphyxiate."

"Now what?" I said. "Is there another way to the generator room?"

Murdock shook his head. "Just this and the main dorsal corridor. Unless we want to go EVA and cut through the hull with a torch, but that's not an option. Their ship sensors would pick up any external movement."

"Maybe we can wait here until he passes," I said.

"There's not enough time," said Murdock. "The Socials will start killing the crew as soon as they have control of the ship. If we wait here for more than an hour, we might be the only ones left."

"Then what do we do?" I said.

"Climb down the ladder and see how many are down there," said Murdock, much to my disbelief.

I just stared at him.

"You're lighter than I am," he pointed out. "You'll make less noise."

He had a point. I didn't like it, but it was still a good one. I sighed, made sure the second pistol's safety was on, and it jammed it into my belt to join the other. Then I gripped the ladder and went down a few rungs, and then kicked my legs out, bracing my boots against the sides of the shaft while my hands held a rung. It was like some sort of dangerous workout position, and I couldn't hold it for very long, but it did permit me to look down into the next deck's maintenance walkway without anyone seeing me.

I saw the back of the commando a dozen feet away. The man stood motionless, his K7 still cradled in his arms. I couldn't hear anything coming out of his helmet, but I had the distinct impression he was listening to something over his radio. Maybe Ducarti was giving a speech. Or maybe he was listening to his favorite ship-boarding tunes, I don't know.

I pulled myself back into the maintenance walkway.

"There's just the one," I said. "He's facing the other way. I think he's getting orders from someone."

Murdock nodded. "All right. Set your pistol to maximum." He shut off the safety on his gun and turned a dial, and I followed suit. A little readout on the back on the gun informed me that at maximum power I would only get sixteen shots off before depleting the power. "Aim for his center of mass, and don't stop shooting until he goes down. You take the ladder." I swung back onto the ladder. "I'll drop down." Murdock perched on the edge of the shaft. "Ready?"

My mouth suddenly felt dry as dust.

I managed a nod.

Murdock nodded back. "On three. One. Two…"

I gripped my pistol in my right hand, my left holding a rung of the ladder.

"Three!"

I slid down the ladder and Murdock jumped. He landed into the next level about a second before I did, his boots clanging against the grillwork of the floor. The Social Party commando heard it loud and clear, and he spun, bringing up his K7 rifle to fire.

A lot of things happened in a very short time and space, and I remember all of them as clear as day.

I swung my gun towards the commando and fired. A laser-burst pistol is silent, has no recoil, and issues an invisible blast, but firing a handgun while hanging one-handed from a ladder isn't exactly ideal accuracy. My first blast missed him, and I knew it missed him because a patch of the inner hull behind him glowed white-hot from my gun's discharge.

Murdock had more skill, or maybe better luck. His first shot hit the commando in the right hip, and the ceramic armor there burned away with a flare of hot fire. The commando staggered, which saved our lives because it threw off his aim. The burst of full-auto gunfire that he directed at us would have cut us in half instead of splattering harmlessly against the wall behind us.

I'd dropped to the walkway and was now in a proper shooting stance, one knee down, both hands rapped around the pistol's grip, just the way Nelson had taught me in his endless security drills. I squeezed the trigger again, and this time the blast burned through the armor on the commando's stomach. Murdock had recovered his balance, and he shot once more, the blast hitting the commando in the chest. I squeezed my trigger a third time, and another hole in the armor appeared next to the one Murdock had made.

One of the blasts had burned through the armor and through the commando's heart. He staggered forward, bounced off the inner hull, and fell upon his face.

I had just killed my first man. Or helped kill him, anyway, which was the same thing.

I know you're supposed to feel bad when you kill someone, that it's supposed to be a shattering experience that gives you nightmares and regrets and maybe post-traumatic stress disorder, but I didn't feel any of that. I mostly felt furious that he'd shot at us, and annoyed that my first shot had missed him. I suppose I should have felt bad that I had killed someone, but let's be real. If he had been given the chance, he would have shot me in the head and not blinked an eye, and for all we knew, his friends were getting ready to murder the entire crew.

"Here," said Murdock, passing me a black pistol he had taken from the dead commando. "Better firepower. We're going to need it." The gun was a lot heavier than my burst laser pistol, probably because it held actual projectiles instead of a capacitator. I didn't know how many rounds a gun like that held. Twenty? However, the safety lever and the trigger were in the same place, so I figured I could use it.

"The collision alarm," I said as Murdock helped himself to the dead man's K7.

"Exactly," said Murdock. "Those rounds hitting the hull will have showed up in the system just the same as debris hitting from the outside. That's hard-wired into the system, and even Williams couldn't lock it out."

"Which means," I said, "they know exactly where we are now."

Murdock nodded. "Move. And stop pointing that thing at me! Last thing I need right now is to get shot in the back."

We hurried down the walkway, the metal grill clanking, the gun's grip cold and heavy against my hands. At last we came to a T-junction, and Murdock went left around the corner. The corridor terminated in another ladder. If I remembered the ship's layout properly, we just had to climb up, make our way twenty or thirty meters to the generator room, and Murdock could do a hard reboot of the computer system.

He came to a stop.

I started to ask what was wrong, and then I heard the noises coming from above. Boots clanked on the deck, and I heard the sharp metallic clank as the end of a gun bounced off the wall.

Someone had noticed the collision alarm, and sent more than one Social to investigate.

Murdock spat out a furious curse, raised his K7 up the ladder shaft, and started shooting. The gun's chattering roar sounded deafening in the enclosed space, the muzzle flash throwing stark shadows against the maze of wiring and pipes on the wall. I heard someone shout above, and then something metallic bounced off the floor near my foot. It was a cylinder of black metal about four inches long, capped on either end, and the commando we had killed had been carrying a bunch of them.

Grenade.

My first thought was that the idiots were going to blast open a massive hull breach.

My second thought was that the grenade was going to blast open a massive hull breach right after it had finished ripping me to bloody shreds.

I drew back my foot to kick the grenade away, hopefully further down the maintenance walkway.

There was a brilliant flash, and a noise so loud that I seemed to feel it across my entire body. Then something hard slammed into my back and the back of my head, and I realized that I had just hit the wall with considerable force.

I felt the metal grillwork of the floor pressing into my face, and then everything went black.

Chapter 5

Hardball Negotiation from the Weaker Position

I was pretty hazy for a while after that.

I think I dreamed. Like, fever dreams, you know? Everything was all disjointed and out of place. For a while I thought Sergei and I were working on the *Rusalka's* maintenance drones, except that didn't make sense because Sergei was dead and had been dead before I had ever set foot upon her.

Then I was talking to my mother. We were standing at a colony *Rusalka* had visited a few trips back, a hellish desert world only habitable near the poles. She stood in the blazing sun and was eagerly lecturing me about the future, but then, without warning, she melted in the sun, her skin and muscle and fat turning to burning slime and sliding from her bones. She stood in front of me, still talking, even though she was nothing but a blackened skeleton. Then the desert caught fire, burning the way that building in New Chicago had burned the day the bomb had gone off, and I heard her screaming for me out of the flames.

I screamed with her.

There were a half-dozen more nightmares. I don't remember them all, which is probably just as well. For a while I had the sensation of floating. Or I was being carried. Maybe the explosion that had killed Mom and Sergei and God knows how many others had thrown me into the air and I was flying… until I crashed into ground and splattered like a package of hamburger dropped from a balcony. For a while, I was convinced that Ducarti's bomb had also destroyed the *Rusalka*, that the ship was careening out of control into one of NR8965's stars, which was why I felt so hot.

Then I felt something cool and hard underneath me. It felt nice.

Angry voices began to echo in my ears, which was rather less nice. It seemed someone was having a loud argument nearby, accompanied by a lot of cursing. I heard something beeping. An instrument panel? No, I recognized the sounds. They were from the various stations on the bridge. That was it. I was lying on the metal floor of the ship's bridge.

One of the angry voices got louder. Maybe they were angry that the ship had crashed into the star and melted the crew? That didn't make sense.

"Where is the key?" said a man's voice. That didn't make any sense either, but after a moment my scrambled brain recognized the voice. It belonged to Thomas Williams, the captain of the *Rusalka*… and the Social Party traitor.

"What are you talking about, you moron?" snarled another voice. It sounded like John Murdock. "What key? You locked the computer yourself. The boy doesn't even know who he is! Look at him!"

Wait. Murdock was dead. He had gone into the maintenance walkway, and one of the commandos had thrown a grenade down the ladder shaft. The explosion in that enclosed space would have killed him.

And me. I remembered that I had been with him. The grenade exploded right near me. That meant I should be dead, too. Only, as near as I could tell, I wasn't.

Huh. Guess that had been a stun grenade, not a fragmentation one.

Then the memories of what had led up to the explosion rushed back into my head, and I couldn't help groaning. Everything hurt. With some effort, I forced my eyes open.

I was right. I was lying on the deck, and I really was on the *Rusalka's* bridge. I saw four Social commandos standing guard, as motionless as statues in their combat armor, their black facemasks reflecting the blinking lights from the bridge consoles. Hawkins and the other bridge crewers were on their knees, their hands held behind their heads. They were all lined up in a row; one long burst from a K7 could kill them all, one after the other. Murdock was kneeling away from the others, and Captain Williams stood over him, a projectile pistol in his right hand and a look of livid fury on his face.

"Tell me," snapped Williams, "where it is!"

Murdock gave him a scornful look. "You're the one who locked the ship's systems. You want access to something, go unlock it yourself."

Williams snarled and hit Murdock across the face with his free hand. Murdock's head snapped around, some blood flying from his mouth. He blinked a few times and looked up at the captain.

"Is that the hardest you can hit?" he said. "You should have spent more time in the gym."

Williams's face went red behind his graying beard, and he leveled his gun at Murdock's forehead. "I'm not playing around. Where is it?"

"For God's sake," said Murdock. "I can't believe I'm going to die because you're too stupid to understand basic computer concepts. You locked the systems. If anyone has the key to unlock it, you do."

"Not that key," said Williams. "I want the key to the grain!"

Murdock blinked. "You mean the cargo bay? It's not hard. You can probably even force the bay with the computer locked."

Williams let out an aggravated sound. "That's not what I meant and you know it. What is the key to the grain? I know you and Rovio were part of a reactionary anti-Party cell. So tell me the key to the grain?"

"It's just grain, you idiot!" said Murdock. "You plant it. Or you grind it up into flour and turn it into bread and stuff. I have no idea what you're babbling about!" He glared at the captain. "How drunk did you get before you sold us all out anyway?"

Williams stepped back, his fingers tightening against the gun, and he might have shot Murdock then and there, but then he saw me looking at him.

"He's awake!" he shouted. "Alesander, the young one woke up! Maybe he'll know!"

I jerked upright to a sitting position, my head swimming, and braced my hands against the deck to keep from falling over. Williams shifted his pistol to point at me, as did one of the commandos.

"Um, hi," I said uncertainly. "Don't shoot."

"That will rather depend," said a familiar voice with a rolling accent, "on what you say in the next five minutes."

I turned my aching head, and Alesander Ducarti swaggered into my line of sight.

He was dressed better than anyone else on the bridge, but more for movie combat than the real thing. He was wearing combat boots, cargo pants, tactical vest, and a leather jacket, but they all looked brand new. He was carrying a lot of weapons too, with pistols on both hips, grenades on his harness, and a K7 slung over his shoulder. His head was tilted to the side, as if in speculation, and his dark eyes looked amused as they stared at me.

"He's Corbin's brat," said Williams, walking to Ducarti's side. Despite his paunch, Williams was a tall and imposing man. Nevertheless, he sort of hovered at Ducarti's elbow, almost like a teenage girl meeting her favorite rock star for the first time. "He's Corbin's little pet."

"Nephew," said Ducarti absently.

"What?" said Williams, blinking.

"The correct term is nephew," said Ducarti. "A sibling's child. In this case, a brother's."

"That's my point," said Williams, puffing up as if he had done something useful. "He's family. Corbin will have told him everything."

"Indeed?" said Ducarti. "Well, then. Do tell us everything, Nikolai."

I took a deep breath. "My name is Nikolai Rovio, and I am an apprentice crewer aboard Starways Hauling Company freighter *Rusalka*, registry number…"

"Yes, yes," said Ducarti with a smile. "I am quite familiar with the formalities, thank you. But we are old acquaintances, are we not, Nikolai? Surely we can speak candidly."

"All right." I glared at him. "Fine. You're a murderer. You killed my mother and my brother."

"Nonsense," said Ducarti. "They killed themselves. No one forced them to do anything."

"You killed them," I spat. "You murdered them and a lot of other people all for your stupid Revolution!"

Williams bristled. "Watch your mouth, boy!"

"Now, now, Captain," said Ducarti with perfect calm. "We already know that young Nikolai and his uncle are reactionaries. Which means that it is possible that Nikolai knows everything that we need to know."

"I'm not telling you anything," I said.

It was pure bluster, and we both knew it. I had heard about the kind of things Social operatives did to their prisoners, the drugs and the neural jammers and the more conventional methods of torture. If Ducarti wanted, he could force me to tell him anything and leave me a physical and mental cripple in the process.

I had a feeling he would enjoy that.

"Let's find out, shall we?" said Ducarti. "Where is the key to the harvest? Tell me where it is, and you may well save the lives of all of your crewmates."

"I don't know what you're talking about," I said in all honesty. "How can a harvest have a key?"

Williams snarled and punched me in the face. It wasn't much of a punch. I guess he never had the benefit of a big brother teaching him how to fight. Nevertheless, I wasn't ready for it, so it was enough to knock me backwards to the deck.

"Belay that, Captain," said Ducarti, strolling forward. "There is no need for violence. Mr. Rovio is going to tell us everything he knows about the *Rusalka's* mission. Then we shall determine whether or not that information is useful, or if

Mr. Rovio himself is useful to us." He put a hand on Williams's shoulder, and the captain stepped to the side.

"Ducarti!" said Hawkins. "If you're going to interrogate anyone, interrogate me. An apprentice crewer won't know anything about the cargo!"

"Do be quiet, Mr. Hawkins," said Ducarti. "Now. Nikolai. Tell me all about the ship's cargo."

I glared up at him. "You know about it already."

"In your own words, please," said Ducarti. "Indulge me."

I wasn't obliged to tell him anything but my name, my rank, and the designation of the ship upon which I served. But I knew that the Social Party did not bother with legal niceties, and Ducarti had absolutely no compunctions about killing me or anyone else. At least if I kept talking, I could keep him from killing me out of hand.

"It's grain," I said. "A whole lot of grain from the colony on New Sibersk."

"So far, so good," said Ducarti. "Now. What is special about New Sibersk? Backwater worlds, after all, are by definition quite common."

"It was founded by people from Novorossiya III," I said. "Refugees. Who fled Novorossiya III after you guys wrecked the place."

Ducarti lifted his eyebrows. "We did not 'wreck the place', as you so vulgarly put it. We brought the Revolution to Novorossiya III and prepared to transition it to a true classless and equal society."

"Yeah," I said. "You're classless, all right."

Ducarti only sniffed dismissively at the feeble insult. "We were making excellent progress. Those who fled to New Sibersk were reactionaries and wreckers, saboteurs meddling with the advance of the Revolution."

"Then the Social government on Novorossiya III got overthrown," I said.

"Alas," said Ducarti, "it appears that the people of Novorossiya III were simply not enlightened enough to appreciate that the hour of the true classless society had come. They shall learn, in time." He made an impatient little flipping gesture with his right hand. "Now, why do you think the Social Party is so interested in their grain?"

"Because you want to screw with the colony on New Sibersk," I said. "They sank a lot of money into producing this harvest, and it's all on this ship. If you steal the grain, you can hurt your enemies and make a big production about the Revolution striking back and all that nonsense. And my guess is your own people are probably starving because they can't even feed themselves."

Williams bristled again. He really seemed enthusiastic about the Social Party. Maybe he thought it would annoy his brother. Ducarti gestured, and once again the captain subsided.

"It is true that I seek to harm the enemies of the Revolution," said Ducarti, "but you are overlooking the obvious. If we simply wanted to destroy New Sibersk's harvest, it would be easier to simply shoot down the *Rusalka*. Or now that we have control of the ship, to steer her into the nearby red giant. But we have done neither of those things. Why?"

"You tell me," I said.

Ducarti smiled. "Let us see if you can figure it out on your own, Nikolai Rovio."

"Games?" I said. "Really? You want to play games?"

Ducarti shrugged. "Or I could just shoot you."

Okay. Maybe a game wasn't so bad.

I realized the sick bastard was enjoying this and another realization followed that. Toying with me instead of finishing his mission, whatever it was, was a mistake. But he needed to feed that oversized ego, and the more I played along, the more time I bought for the others on the ship to do something.

"All right," I said. "I'm in. So it's not about the grain. Or it's not just about the grain. Blowing up New Sibersk's grain harvest is just a bonus."

"Go on," said Ducarti.

"Like, there are a hundred thousand people on New Sibersk," I said. "The colony might fail on its own. There are billions of people on Social Party planets and even a big harvest like this won't feed them all. You can't care that much about New Sibersk. I mean, you'll kill them or impoverish them if you get the chance, but you have bigger things on your mind."

"Interesting," said Ducarti. "Do continue, Mr. Rovio. You may be even more clever than your late parents."

A bolt of sheer rage flashed through me, and I wanted to get up and strangle him until I squeezed that smug look off his face. Only the certain knowledge that his commandos would shoot me dead before I even touched him kept me from doing it.

"If wrecking the harvest is only a side project," I said, "that means you have some other reason for taking the ship. You could have just blown up the ship, but you didn't. You boarded it. So either you want the ship itself, or there's something on the ship you want."

I frowned as I realized it must be the latter. There was nothing special about *Rusalka* except her size.

"There is something you want," I said, "but something you can't get. Because the captain kept asking for a key."

"Precisely," said Ducarti. "Now, Mr. Rovio. Where is this key?"

I shrugged. "I don't know what's locked up. Williams can unlock anything in the computer. If there's something physically locked up, you've probably got plasma torches. So it's something trickier than that."

"Correct," said Ducarti. "We are not discussing a physical or a digital lock." He seemed to consider something for a moment. "Tell me. Are you familiar with noncoding DNA?"

"What?" I said. I had no idea what he was talking about.

"More colloquially known as junk DNA," said Ducarti. "Surely you must have sat through a biology course at some point."

"We're talking about biology now?" I said, baffled. "Okay, if I remember right, every cell has DNA, which is the instructions for making more cells. Except not all of the DNA gets used because it's full of mutations and stuff. That's the junk DNA. It's like a bunch of old temporary files on a hard drive that never get erased and just sort of sit there taking up space."

"A crude, but sufficient summary," said Ducarti. "As you said, junk DNA is mostly useless, but among the scientists of the Thousand Worlds there are scientists clever enough to alter the junk DNA."

"So what?" I said. "Genetic engineering has been a science since… I don't even know. Since before people left Earth's solar system for the first time."

"Indeed," said Ducarti. "And the grain from New Sibersk has not been genetically altered in any significant way, save for the alterations made millennia ago to weed out certain diseases and promote good health and so forth. Yet the scientists on New Sibersk have employed a specific genetic engineering technique to hide altered code within the junk DNA of their grain."

"That's where the information you want is," I said. "In the grain."

"Precisely," said Ducarti. "The grain contains a list of names required by the revolution."

"Decryption. You need the decryption key, because you can't read it otherwise."

"In a word, yes," said Ducarti.

"Whose names?" I said. "More people you plan to kill?"

"I'm afraid the situation is far more serious than that," said Ducarti. "No, as it happens, this is a list of our friends."

"You jerks have friends?" I said.

"Many," said Ducarti. "The Revolution has freed only a small number of worlds. Yet the governments and corporations of many other worlds are home to those who are friendly to the cause of the Revolution. Captain Williams, for one." Williams beamed as if that was a compliment. "Naturally, should their true affiliations become known, our friends will be at grave risk."

"Which is to say they'll be arrested for treason."

"So we undertake great efforts to conceal their identities," said Ducarti. "Unfortunately. New Sibersk has become a haven for reactionaries and others opposed to the glorious goals of the Revolution. Among them is a former intelligence officer who happened to possess a list of our friends, which he then encoded into the grain."

"That's stupid," I said. "Why put the list in junk DNA? Why not just encode it into a virus and propagate it?"

"That is the first smart thing you've said, boy," said Williams. "All who oppose the Revolution are stupid."

"Alas," said Ducarti, "would that they were. The reactionaries exhibit a sort of base cunning. We know New Sibersk is a nest of reactionaries and class traitors. We know that several of our former intelligence officers have taken shelter there, and hidden traitors and wreckers within the Social Party have been sending them information. So naturally we have been monitoring all communications in and out, and watching all vessels arriving and departing from the colony."

"We should have nuked the place from orbit," said Williams.

"The traitors on New Sibersk could not broadcast their information as you suggested, for we would then find them and have them liquidated. We could not take hostile action against New Sibersk without triggering a war. So some clever person among our enemies had the idea of slipping the list into the junk DNA of the grain harvest. That way, the list could be smuggled out with ease. The identities of our friends in high places would be exposed, and many would be ruined, imprisoned, or executed. This would be a grievous blow to the progress of the Revolution."

I looked at Williams. "You told him, didn't you?"

Williams smirked. "I am proud to do my part for the Revolution."

"And to piss off your brother, right?" I said. That made the smirk vanish from his face. I looked back at Ducarti, hoping Williams wouldn't hit me again. "So what do you need a key for? There are hundreds of thousands of tons of grain in the hold. Go get some grain and decode it."

"Alas," said Ducarti, "decryption is no longer a simple matter of brute computing force. We have already begun the process, but it could take years." He smiled. "But you, Mr. Rovio, are going to provide me with that key and save me that time."

"Just how am I going to do that?"

"Because your uncle almost certainly has a hand in all of this," said Ducarti. "Corbin Rovio is a reactionary traitor. Your father, at least, held true to the ideals of the Revolution, even if he got himself killed in their execution. Corbin Rovio, though… it seems Corbin was always a traitor."

I shook my head. "You're wasting your time. My uncle didn't tell me anything." That annoyed me a little. On the other hand, I supposed he had been protecting me, or at least trying to.

Fat lot of good that did me now. Assuming, of course, he had really known about this, and Ducarti wasn't lying.

"I didn't know about any of this. I couldn't even remember what junk DNA was until I thought about it. I'm just an apprentice technician."

"True, but even if Corbin did not confide in you, he will not wish to watch you suffer. Once we have him, he will talk."

"I know my uncle. And he knows you. He'll die before he lets you take him. And he'll let me die before he'll give in to you!"

"You may be right," admitted Ducarti. "He hasn't responded to any of our broadcasts in which I clearly spelled out what the consequences would be." He lifted his hand to his right ear, tapping the earpiece that he wore. He spoke a few words in a soft voice, and then turned to the waiting commandos. "Sergeant, we're going to have to search the ship from bow to stern. We need to root out any crew members who are still in hiding. Also, I want Corbin Rovio alive."

The blast door to the corridor hissed open, and a pair of commandos strode inside, K7 rifles at the ready.

"So, it is time to make good our threats," said Ducarti. He pointed at me and then at Murdock. "Take them both and throw them out the rear airlock."

"What?" said Murdock.

"That is a violation of interstellar law…" started Hawkins.

"Reactionary nonsense," said Ducarti. "Besides, you'll be pleased to know that we do not intend to shoot anyone, Mr. Hawkins. Why make a mess we will only have to clean up? The vacuum of space will provide a much cleaner death. And a more painful one as well."

"You sick—" started Hawkins, but one of the commandos silenced him with an armored backhand.

The other commando grabbed my arms and hauled me to my feet, handcuffing my wrists behind my back. His partner did the same for Murdock, who let out a steady stream of profanity.

"You traitorous rat," said Murdock to Williams. "You're going to just stand there with that stupid expression on your face and let him execute your crew one by one?"

Williams smirked. "You're enemies of the Revolution. You made your choice."

The commandos looked at Ducarti.

"Proceed, gentlemen," he said. Then he turned around, without so much as a parting sneer at me or Murdock. He really was a cold-hearted bastard.

The two commandos hustled me and Murdock to our feet, herded us out the blast door to the main dorsal corridor, and pushed us along.

Later, this was the part that gave me nightmares.

Not shooting that one commando in the maintenance walkways. Not all the other stuff that happened. Walking down that corridor, just walking with my hands behind my back, was the part that gave me bad dreams. Knowing that I was slowly, inexorably, getting marched to my death and that there was nothing I could do to stop it, nothing at all… that leaves a mark on your mind.

I still wake up shaking from it sometimes.

Death by vacuum isn't really a fun way to go. I won't describe all the grisly details, but if you've ever seen corpses pulled in from vacuum, there's a reason they look like they died in agony. As painful as that was, death by radiation burns was much worse. And the direction they were taking us, towards the rear airlock, would jettison us fatally close to the ship's drive.

There was a reason the sublight drive had all kinds of armor and shielding around it. At least it would be quick. The lack of air would kill me before the drive radiation finishing cooking my innards like a cheap meal in a microwave oven. A few months ago I had tried to eat a frozen burrito for lunch, and had hit the wrong buttons on the microwave in the technicians' lounge. The thing had exploded all over the inside of the microwave, and Corbin had made sure my task for the next week was to repair every microwave oven on the ship.

I wondered if I would explode like that burrito.

I was so scared, definitely the most scared I had ever been in my much-too-short life.

We reached the end of the dorsal corridor, with the doors to the engineering section on the right. The rear airlock waited at the end of the corridor. Murdock let out a steady stream of furious curses, and I realized that he was going to attack the commandos, even with his hands bound behind his back. That would be suicide, but getting shot through the forehead by a K7 round was a quicker and less painful way to die than asphyxiation accompanied by radiation poisoning. And wasn't it better to go out fighting? If I was going to die, I would rather die fighting than begging for my life.

I had one last thought. I don't know if there's an afterlife or not, and I had never given religion much thought. The Social Party was entirely atheist, and they're wrong about everything else, so I assume there must be a God. So, if I saw my mom and Sergei in the afterlife, I would finally get to tell them "I told you so" about Alesander Ducarti.

Cold comfort, that.

We stopped before the airlock. The commando guarding me stuck his rifle's muzzle into the small of my back. With his free hand he reached over and hit the airlock control. The control panel flashed, and the inner door slid open with a quiet hiss. Beyond it I saw the thick gray metal of the outer door, all that separated us from the vacuum of space and the lethal radiation coming from the *Rusalka's* drive.

"Inside, now," said the commando.

I hesitated, and the commando gave me a sharp jab with his rifle. It's really hard to keep your balance with your hands bound behind your back, and I stumbled forward and bounced off the frame of the inner door.

"You, too," said the second commando, stepping back several steps and leveling his K7 at Murdock. One good burst from the rifle would kill Murdock and me, or leave us bleeding to death in the airlock.

Murdock tensed, and I realized that he was about to attack them. I braced myself to follow suit. I hoped the commandos would shoot us in the head and make it quick. Of course, they could also just shoot us in the knees or the stomach. Then the commandos could drag us into the airlock and let us enjoy a few extra moments of agony until we died.

"Last chance to die like men," said the second commando. "Now get in there yourselves, or we'll do it the hard way."

The commando jerked, and the nasty smell of burning armor flooded my nose. The commandos whirled, raising his rifle, and then both men fell. The second man got off a burst of gunfire that ricocheted off the hull a few inches from my left leg. Smoke rose from the prone commandos, the stench of melted armor mixing with the greasier odor of charred flesh.

Someone had just cooked them both with lasers.

The door to the engineering room had opened, and I saw my uncle standing there with a laser pistol in his hand. Security Chief Nelson stood next to him, scowling at the dead commandos, and three of Corbin's techs were with him, all armed.

I was too weak with relief to say anything.

"About time," said Murdock sourly.

"Either of you hurt?" said Corbin.

I managed to shake my head. "No. Just a bit foggy from the stun grenade."

"Excellent," said Nelson. "That gives us two more combat effectives."

"And two less for them is plus four in all. It's a mutiny, gentlemen," said Corbin. "We're going to take back the ship from Williams and Ducarti. Care to join us?"

"Oh, God, yes!" I said.

Chapter 6

Automated Cargo Handling For Fun And Profit

Nelson and Corbin searched the dead commandos, stripping them of their weapons with practiced movements. After a moment Corbin produced a key from one of the commandos' belts, and undid our handcuffs. They were mechanical handcuffs, not electronic. I suppose that made them more secure. It's a lot harder to hack a good mechanical lock than something electronic. You would literally need a hacksaw or a cutting laser to cut through a metal lock.

My thoughts were bouncing all over the place. The aftereffects of the adrenaline, I suppose. That, and escaping certain death.

"Here you go, son," said Nelson, handing me one of the dead commandos' machine pistols. Nelson didn't smile as he said it. I suspected he called everyone under the age of fifty "son".

"Thanks," I said, making sure the safety was on. I took a deep breath, trying to get my racing heart and rapid breathing under control. I suddenly felt the need to throw up, and once again I was grateful I hadn't eaten anything today. If I puked on Nelson's boots, he would probably recite every regulation relating to the disposal of shipboard biohazards, and I didn't want to listen to that right now.

"So," said Murdock. He helped himself to one of the dead commandos' K7 rifles. "I think I have a question or two for you, Corbin."

"I imagine so," said Corbin. He glanced at me. "You too, Nikolai."

"Yeah," I said. "Ducarti was asking us about junk DNA and lists of secret agents hidden in the grain. Was he telling the truth, or is he chasing a red herring?"

"Not here," said Corbin, glancing along the corridor. Far in the distance, nearly a kilometer down the dorsal corridor, I could see the closed blast doors that sealed off the bridge. If Ducarti realized what had happened, he could simply open the doors and spray gunfire down the corridor until we were all dead. "Engineering room. We'll be safer there."

"Will we?" I said. I supposed Ducarti wouldn't want to start shooting in the engineering room, given all the various machines and devices that could explode. Shooting a conduit of coolant or drive plasma is a really, really bad idea.

"Given that I've rigged the hypermatter reactor to explode, yes," said Corbin.

Murdock and I stared at him.

"How is that safer?" I said at last.

"What?" said Murdock.

"Come on," said Corbin. "This isn't the place to talk about it. Wait, Nikolai—grab his helmet. We might need it in a few minutes."

I shrugged and pulled off the helmet of the nearest dead commando. The face beneath the mask was slack, the eyes glassy and staring. I suppose I should have felt something, a pang of emotion, a flicker of feeling at our shared mortality, but the guy had been planning shove me out an airlock to die, so I was just glad not to be in his place.

"Move, people," snapped Nelson, keeping his newly acquired K7 pointed towards the distant bridge blast doors. I tucked the helmet under one arm and followed Murdock and Corbin and the other techs towards the engineering doors. A mass of wires dangled from the doors' control panel.

"Computer lockout," said Corbin in response to the unanswered question. "The captain sealed the doors to the engineering section. So we ripped out the network connection and used the manual override."

Murdock grunted. "Bet it made a lot of noise."

"It did," said Corbin. "Of course, we knew it would, so Mr. Nelson and a few of the techs laid an ambush. When four of Ducarti's commandos showed up, we surprised them and relieved them of their lives and their weapons."

"It was regulation-smooth," said Nelson, which was probably the highest compliment he had for anything.

We headed into the engineering room. It was a big room, twice as large as the bridge, and stuffed with consoles and instrument tables. At the moment, all of the consoles and instrument tables showed the same SYSTEM LOCKED message I had seen in the computer room and the bridge. Nelson dispatched two of the techs to guard the doors back to the dorsal corridor. Both men had K7 rifles taken from dead commandos, and anyone trying to force their way into the engine room would meet a hail of gunfire.

"All right," said Murdock. "I think you've got some questions to answer, Corbin."

"Yeah," I said. "Like junk DNA and secret agents."

"First things first," said Murdock, cutting me off, "Are you really going to blow up the ship, Rovio?"

"I hope not," said Corbin. He reached into a pocket of his jacket and drew out a flat black box. "Nikolai. Recognize this?"

My head was still aching and it took a moment to get my brain into focus. "That is a… reinforced computer processor. Shielded against EMP pulses and radiation and stuff like that." Some of the charts I had memorized for my certification tests swam up to the forefront of my thoughts. "There's only a few of them on the ship. So that means…"

I blinked. Then I swallowed. Hard.

Murdock let out a few curses. Somehow, he never seemed to repeat himself.

"You took that out of the regulator on the hypermatter re-actor," I said, resisting the urge to send a nervous glance at the metal deck beneath my feet. "That means the reactor is destabilizing, right now!"

"It will explode," said Corbin, tucking the processor back into his pocket. "Eventually. Not for another six to nine hours, though. It will take that long for the hypermatter reaction to destabilize sufficiently."

"What good does that do us?" said Murdock. "You do know we're actually on the ship you're blowing up, don't you?"

"Oh," I said as the realization came to me.

"Explain it for Murdock," said Corbin with a faint smile. "Computer guys deal with software, and they aren't used to the nuts and bolts of the real world."

Murdock scowled. "I'll tell you what you can do with your nuts and bolts."

"If two operating hypermatter reactors get too close to each other," I said, recalling the prep material for the certification test, "they can become entangled on a quantum level. Like… tachyons, that's it. The regulator is supposed to keep that from happening. Except Corbin pulled out the regulator's processor while the hypermatter reactor on Ducarti's ships are still running."

"Which means," Corbin broke in, "that when our reactor goes up, the reactors on the *Vanguard* and the troop transport will go as well. Doesn't matter how far they run, or even if they make it to hyperspace. Once two hypermatter reactors are entangled, if one goes, they both go."

"Wonderful," I said. I suppose it would be poetic justice if Ducarti was blown up unawares, just as he had done to my mother and brother. I didn't particularly want to blow up with him, though.

"Fine," said Murdock. "So we're going to particulate in nine hours unless you put that processor back into the regulator. But what about the rest of it, Rovio? Ducarti seems to think that there's some sort of secret list of Social Party agents encoded into the junk DNA of the grain shipment."

There was silence for a moment.

"He's not wrong," my uncle finally said.

Murdock swore loudly and threw his hands up. "I don't mind the dangerous cargoes. But cloak-and-dagger nonsense, Rov? I thought you had left the military. We all did!" He waved a hand in my direction. "What's next, you'll tell me that the kid is actually a trained infiltrator or something?"

"I don't understand," I said.

"What Mr. Rovio just said, although not in so many words," explained Murdock, still steaming, "is that he's an intelligence officer with the Coalition navy."

"Really?" I said.

"I'm afraid so," said Corbin.

"And you never told me?" I said.

"The point of being a secret intelligence officer," said Corbin, "is not to tell anyone, though I expect it's a little late at this point. After I finished my term in the navy, the intel division recruited me. The main focus of Coalition intelligence for years has been the Social Party, and as you can imagine, I have something of a grudge against the bastards. Working for Starways gives me an excellent excuse to travel around the Thousand Worlds, and there are always little errands that need doing here and there."

Murdock's eyes narrowed. "Wet work? Black ops? Offing agents of the Revolution?"

Corbin didn't blink. "Sometimes. If need be. Not often, though. Killing a man usually makes a bigger mess than just leaving suspicious funds in his account, or delivering the contents of his phone to the local police."

"All right," said Murdock. "So this business with the list encoded in the junk DNA. Was this your mission?"

"Not originally," said Corbin. "Some of the exiles on New Sibersk thought it up. The colony is mostly refugees from Novorossiya III, from when the revolutionary government went berserk and began the mass executions before it finally collapsed. Consequently, exiles and refugees from other worlds the Social Party has trashed tend to wind up there. Some of them were former members of the Socials' intelligence and secret police apparatuses, and they had a lot of information their former higher-ups didn't want falling into the wrong hands."

"So why junk DNA?" I said. "That seems like a horribly over-complicated way to do it. Why not send an email? Why not just write it down on a piece of paper and mail it the old-fashioned way?"

"Politics," said Corbin.

Murdock groaned. "Oh, for God's sake. Always with the politics. This is why I got out of the navy, you know."

"The situation is complicated," said Corbin, "but to sum it up, the Social Party can't attack New Sibersk without drawing serious repercussions, nor can any of the Party's clients or proxies. Furthermore, the Party knows that some of its sensitive information has been lost… but it doesn't know how much of it, so the Reds haven't really been able to prepare. They've been spying on New Sibersk for years, so the exiles don't dare to send the list out electronically. A paper copy can be stolen or destroyed. So some of the exiles hit on the idea of encoding the list in the junk DNA of the grain harvest."

"Why junk DNA?" I said.

"Because the Social Party lacks the scientific expertise to decode it," said Corbin.

"Really?" I said. "Why?"

Corbin's cold smile held no mirth. "Because a few years ago, they purged most of their competent geneticists for political disloyalty after a failed harvest."

"Typical," said Murdock with a contemptuous snort.

"We arranged for Starways to get the contract for the harvest," said Corbin, "and for the harvest to go aboard the *Rusalka*. The easiest solution for the Social Party's problem was to simply blow up the ship, but the *Rusalka* has the armaments of a small capital warship, and the blockade runners and stealth frigates the Socials use on missions like this wouldn't have a prayer against her guns. In a straight fight, the *Rusalka* would have blasted the *Vanguard* and the troop transport out of the sky in about a minute."

"Except," I said, "you didn't know that Williams was Social."

"Or did you know that he was one of them?" said Murdock, a dangerous edge in his voice.

"I didn't," said Corbin. "I knew he was crooked. I knew he was selling information to some shady agents with Social connections, but he was selling it to anyone who would pay him. That was why I had you and Hawkins keep track of him. I never thought he would leak information that would endanger his own ship to someone like Ducarti. I thought he was corrupt at best and an embezzler at worst. I didn't know he was actually a revolutionary."

"I bet it was Ducarti," I said. "Ducarti sold him on it."

Nelson frowned. "What do you mean?"

"I heard Ducarti speak on New Chicago before the bomb went off," I said. "He's persuasive. I thought he was full of it, but my mom didn't and my brother didn't, and he got both of them killed. The audience for his speech was full of guys like Captain Williams. Fat old professors and bureaucrats with easy enough lives, but they all thought they'd been screwed. Then along comes Ducarti with his big words, and they think they get to be heroes of the revolution or something. He takes advantage of that."

"So why didn't you fall for it?" said Murdock.

"Nothing he said makes sense," I replied. "I mean, engines make sense. Fuel goes in, thrust and power come out. There's no such thing as a free lunch. Everything has to be paid for. Ducarti just talked a lot of nonsense that he made sound good."

"The Socials usually do," said Nelson.

Murdock shook his head. "You should have warned us, Rovio. You shouldn't have gotten us involved in this sort of thing."

"I didn't know it was this sort of thing," said Corbin. He sighed. "If I had known Williams was with the Socials, I wouldn't have risked this. I thought we would just transport the grain to people who could decode it, and that if a trouble-maker like Ducarti showed up, we would blow his ship away. All our lives are at risk, and I'm sorry about that, but right now it's more important to decide what we're going to do to get out of this mess."

"Sure," I said. "So what *are* we going to do now?"

"We start," said Corbin, "by making a phone call. Still got that helmet, Nikolai?"

"Yeah," I said, holding it up. I still had it in my left hand.

"Good," said Corbin. "Nelson, Murdock, watch the door."

"Oh, so you're in charge now?" said Murdock.

Corbin stared him down. "I'm trained for this sort of thing. But if you have any bright ideas, I'm listening."

Murdock stared at him for a moment, then made a rude gesture, but he turned to watch the door back to the dorsal corridor. Nelson did the same, but without comment, complaint, or gesture. Corbin nodded, then knelt next to one of the consoles, pulling open the access panel, and started to disconnect some wires.

"Open up the back of that helmet, Nikolai," said Corbin. "There should be a release latch at the base, and inside you'll see an access jack for the helmet's computer and radio."

I nodded, fumbled with the helmet for a bit, and popped open the access panel. The helmet had a surprising amount of electronics packed into it, including a nanocomputer, a radio, and a HUD for the visor. Corbin passed me a slender cable, and I plugged it into a jack in the helmet's computer. The display on the console flickered, and suddenly switched to a command line interface for the helmet.

"Williams has got the ship's system locked down," said Corbin, typing a string of commands, "so we'll borrow the helmet's computer. There's a scrambler in this console, so when Ducarti gets the call, he won't be able to pinpoint the location… ah, here we go."

He hit a button, and Ducarti's voice crackled over the speakers.

"Report, X-22," he ordered, his irritation plain. "Report in! Have you disposed of the operator and the boy yet? If you have, join the others in cargo bay five. They're having some trouble with the robotics there, and they require reinforcement. Once that's dealt with, we need to find Corbin Rovio. The reactionary is hiding somewhere on the ship–"

"Captain Ducarti! You've found me," said Corbin. "I bet that was easier than you thought. Guess you're historically inevitable after all!"

For a moment there was silence.

"Corbin Rovio," said Ducarti, his voice calm and self-assured. "The traitor himself. You could have risen high in the Party, you know. Your brother, at least, understood the value of loyalty. Had he lived–"

"But he didn't. He blew himself up," said Corbin. "He was loyal to the wrong people."

"I'm sure you know all about that," said Ducarti. "Your nephew just learned that the hard way."

I blinked and looked at Corbin, who raised a finger to his lips.

"What do you mean?" said Corbin.

"He was loyal to you, and he choose poorly," said Ducarti. "Alas, the brave young fool refused to give up your secrets. So I had my men dump him out the stern airlock, right into the drive trail. I understand he begged and screamed for his life until the end."

Corbin gestured to me as Ducarti continued his nasty little monologue. I looked at him and saw him mouth the words "be annoying" while pointing at the console.

Annoying? Right. I definitely could manage that!

"Hey, moron," I addressed the console. "Remember me?"

Ducarti suddenly fell silent.

"I have to ask you one thing," I said. "That accent. All those rolling Rs. Is that fake? I mean, it has to be fake. Do the revolutionary babes fall for that or something? See, I think you're not taking it far enough. Have you ever considered changing it up, you know, just a rrrrittle, for the rrrradies?"

Someone burst out laughing in the background. I wasn't sure if it was Hawkins, a bridge crewer, or one of Ducarti's men.

"Ah, Rovio the Younger" said Ducarti. "I suppose that explains where you got that radio. Ran off to rescue your little nephew, did you? How very bourgeoisie of you, Corbin."

"You can call stopping an attempted murder whatever you like," said Corbin. "But I know you Social Party psychopaths enjoy killing men, women, and children for no reason. If you were sane or competent, you wouldn't have joined the Party. Of course, indulging in your lunatic murder sprees sometimes has unforeseen consequences. If you hadn't killed off all your competent geneticists, we wouldn't be having this conversation..."

"Save your breath," said Ducarti. A little of the smooth polish had come off his voice. "If you're so very keen to save lives, Rovio the Elder, I suggest you surrender yourself and give me the code sequence to the junk DNA. If you don't, I will order my men to start executing your fellow crew members, one every minute, until you come to your senses."

"I wouldn't do that, Ducarti," said Corbin.

"Oh? And just why not?"

"Because I don't know the decryption key," said Corbin. "No one on the ship does. That's just basic operational security, if that isn't too bourgeois for you. Also, I should warn you that you're going to have much bigger problems in about seven hours or so."

"Such as what?" Ducarti demanded, suspicious. He was starting to sound rattled now.

Corbin grinned mercilessly at the console. "You really should have shut down the *Vanguard's* hypermatter reactor. Too late now."

There was silence for a full thirty seconds on the console.

"I see," Ducarti said at last. "Very clever, Rovio. I deduce that you've removed the processor from the *Rusalka's* regulator?"

"We seem to have a bit of standoff," said Corbin. "Boarding a hostile ship with your hyper-reactor still running isn't the greatest idea."

"We will simply shut down our hypermatter reactor," said Ducarti.

I couldn't help but laugh aloud at that. "Good Lord, did you ever even read a technical manual, Ducarti?"

Corbin smiled and gestured for me to continue.

"See, once a hypermatter reactor is entangled, it can't be shut down," I said. "The only way to stop the reaction is to reactivate the regulator on the first reactor, bring it back to the green zone, then shut them both down." I remembered one of the taunts Ducarti had thrown at me back on New Chicago, the day he had murdered my mother and my brother. "If you had bothered to learn the skills of a mere tradesman in service of our oppressive overlords or whatever, you might not have done something so stupid."

"So I have an offer for you," said Corbin. "Evacuate your men back to the *Vanguard* and your troopship and get off the *Rusalka*. Dump your weapons, and move off to a distance of five million kilometers. Then I reinstall the regulator, and you can depart with your lives."

"A fine offer," said Ducarti, some of the mocking poise returning to his voice. "Unfortunately, you have overlooked one small detail. The troopship does not have a hyperdrive, and therefore no hypermatter reactor. We will simply board it and move to a safe distance before both vessels explode."

I blinked. No hyperdrive? Then how had the troopship gotten here? The *Vanguard* must have towed it.

"This system is deserted," said Corbin. "If you blow up both hyperdrive-capable ships in the system, you'll be stranded here a long time before someone finds you. Certainly longer than your supplies and life support will last."

"Another Social Party vessel is scheduled to pass through NR8965 in ten days to check on the status of our mission," said Ducarti. "Ten days is a long time, but we will be long gone before anyone realizes what happened to *Rusalka*. I would, of course, prefer to decode the junk DNA in the hold and learn the identity of our traitors, but destroying the ship will be a satisfactory outcome. Certainly it would cause a great deal of economic distress to the nest of reactionary traitors upon New Sibersk."

"You could simply surrender now and save everyone a lot of trouble," said Corbin. "A lot of lives, too."

Ducarti laughed. "No, Corbin, I need to do nothing at all. You've signed your own death warrant. All I need to do is wait. You may have entangled the hypermatter reactor, but I have control of the *Rusalka's* computer, and without that you can do nothing else. All you can do is wait for the ship to explode. Now goodbye, Corbin Rovio. I leave you to die in the knowledge that the Revolution has defeated you."

The connection ended with a burst of static.

"Well, that was unexpected" I said. "And disappointing. Now what?"

"Yeah, good question," called Murdock from the doors. "Any bright ideas before we all die?"

"I have a plan," said Corbin. I doubt the others believed him any more than I did.

"And if it doesn't work?" said Murdock.

"Then I have a fallback plan," said Corbin.

"That's such a huge relief," I said.

"You're too young to have such a smart mouth, Nikolai" said Corbin. "Listen, all of you. Our first objective is to save our lives. To do that, we have to move fast. We've got to storm the bridge, overpower Ducarti's men there, and take Captain Williams prisoner. Once we have him, we can force him to unlock the computer, and then we can blast the *Vanguard* and the troopship to pieces."

"He won't want to give up the codes," said Nelson.

Murdock snorted. "Then we'll hit him with a wrench until he changes his mind."

"Won't Ducarti just shoot Williams first?" I said.

"Probably," said Corbin. "But Hawkins has some unlock codes that should work once we free him."

"Really?" said Murdock, scowling as he watched the corridor. "I thought only the captain has those codes."

"Normally, yes," said Corbin, "but I have some friends in the home office at Starways, and I persuaded them to give Hawkins more access than usual."

Murdock snorted. "Friends?"

"Ducarti might shoot them both if he realizes it," I said. "He'll kill anyone who gets in his way."

"If he does," said Corbin, "then the backup plan is to kill as many of the commandos as possible and seize control of the *Vanguard* and their troopship. If we do that, I can stabilize our hypermatter reactor and keep the ships from exploding. After that, we'll have to send some men aboard the *Vanguard* to get help, since the computer will still be locked, but we'll have enough supplies to wait here for a long time."

"God knows we have enough grain," I said. "We could grind some flour and make some bread."

"That's pretty thin, Rovio," said Murdock. "They're better armed and armored than we are, and they have control of the ship."

"We have more of us," said Corbin, "and they don't have control of the ship. They've locked the ship, and if they unlock it for any reason, we can get back in with Murdock's access. And we know the ship better."

"Or we'll all get killed," said Murdock.

Corbin shrugged. "Ducarti would kill us all anyway. Are you in or not? If you are, we need to move now."

Murdock blew out a long breath. "It's not as if I have any better ideas. All right, Secret Agent Rovio, what's our move?"

"Hit the bridge, rescue Hawkins, capture Williams, and preferably kill the enemy leadership in the process," said Corbin.

"They've got the dorsal corridor buttoned up pretty tight," said Nelson. "If we try and charge up the corridor to the bridge, they'll mow us down."

"If we go to the ventral corridor," said Murdock, "they'll have men down there securing the sensor arrays and the weapons grid."

"Undoubtedly," said Corbin, "but I doubt they'll have many men in the cargo bays themselves."

"Ducarti said they had a problem in bay five," I said.

"That's the port side of the ship," said Murdock. "We had better take the starboard side."

"Or," said Corbin, "we take the port bays and catch Ducarti's men from behind while they're distracted. Some of the damage control team was down in bay five when Williams locked us out of the computer. If they're holding up Ducarti's men, we have a chance to hit them from behind."

"Aren't the bays in vacuum?" I said.

"They are," said Corbin.

"Wonderful," said Murdock, looking more sour than usual.

"The equipment lockers have suits," said Corbin, "and the locks aren't computer-controlled. We'll cut across bay seven and see what's happening in bay five. Nelson, Murdock. Barricade the doors, and then we'll take the maintenance walkways to the port-side cargo bays. Nikolai, give them a hand getting the doors closed."

Nelson handed me something, and I realized that it was a folded gun belt, with a holster for my stolen machine pistol. I made sure that the safety was on—if I shot myself in the leg with that thing, the bullet would shatter my femur and turn my leg to hamburger. On the plus side, I would bleed to death pretty quickly, but then, it was too soon to give up hope. We still had more than six hours before the ship vaporized, after all.

I donned the belt, holstered the gun, and helped Nelson and Murdock pull the door to the dorsal corridor closed, and then heaped equipment cases in front of it. When Ducarti and his men came to kill us, it would take them at least a few minutes to get through the door. Given the large quantities of flammable and toxic materials flowing through coolant pipes and conduits in the floor and ceiling, I doubted he would dare to use explosives to blow the door open.

Once the door was blocked, we headed single-file into the maintenance walkways. Corbin took the front, and I took the back, not that it would have done me any good. The rounds from those Tanith-Mordecai K7s were designed for use in ships and would fragment upon hitting metal, but would punch through all seven off us without much difficulty. Fortunately, we did not encounter any commandos in the walkways, and after descending three levels, we reached the access airlock to the port side cargo bays.

"Only four of us are going to fit in that airlock at a time," said Murdock.

I opened the equipment locker and started passing out the pressure suits. They weren't that heavy, thanks to their handy carbon-weave material, and would fit over our clothes. Boots and gauntlets had pressure seals, as did the helmet with its clear visor. A heavy pack held the supply of air and the life support equipment. Unfortunately, the suits were bright orange. That helped rescuers find injured crewers in an emergency, but it would also make us easy targets for Ducarti's men.

"I'll go first," said Nelson. "You, you, and you with me." He pointed at the three techs. "We'll make sure the airlock is secure and then bring the others."

We suited up and took a moment to synchronize the suits' radios. Fortunately, each suit had its own on-board computer, disconnected from the main system, so they could still communicate with each other. I pulled on my own suit, following the directions I had memorized in various technical manuals. The gauntlets and the boots locked to the cuffs, producing an airtight seal, and slung my gun belt around my waist, the fake black leather stark against the orange material of the suits. Once I was done, I locked the helmet in place, and the suit booted up. Low-resolution letters and numbers appeared on the suit's cheap HUD, and after a moment, all systems flashed green.

"Ready?" crackled Corbin's voice in my ears.

"Aye aye!" We acknowledged him, and Nelson and the three techs went through the airlock first. Nelson signaled all clear on the other side, so I followed Corbin and Murdock into the airlock. The door closed with a thump, and I felt the humming vibration as the pumps sucked all the air out of the little chamber. A light flashed red on the control panel, and Corbin hit a button.

The door slid open in silence, thanks to the new vacuum, and we stepped into cargo bay seven.

It was huge. Like I've said, the *Rusalka* could carry half a million tons of cargo, and all that cargo had to go somewhere. I've seen pictures of cathedrals upon other worlds, and cargo bay seven looked like a massive cathedral of dull steel, the ceiling far overhead, the walls lined with metal racks. Hundreds of shipping containers filled most of the space, stacked in orderly rows, each one stamped with the official seal of New Sibersk. There was enough grain to feed tens thousands of people for months stacked all around me, and as I looked at it, I felt a flicker of admiration for the exiles on New Sibersk. They had taken their list of Social Party sympathizers and hidden it inside *quadrillions* of kernels of grain upon the ship.

It was a brilliant idea, but it was a pity they hadn't thought to split up the shipment between multiple ships.

"This way," said Corbin. We started down the central aisle, the stacks of shipping containers rising overuse like cubical metal hills. Bright arc lights had been mounted on the ceilings and the walls, but the bay was so vast that the lights only made the place seemed gloomy, as shadows struck curious poses everywhere.

Overhead, bolted to the distant ceiling, hung a variety of tracks and tubes. A massive cargo handling drone hung from the tracks, looking like a giant wasp of black metal. A dozen arms and manipulators of various sizes hung from the underside of the drone, and banks of sensors mounted its sides. When Arthur had them programmed properly, they could zip back and forth from the cargo shuttles to the bay proper, stacking the cargo containers as quickly as I had built towers out of toy bricks when I had been a kid.

Except each bay was supposed to have two cargo drones. One was missing.

I looked down, and saw a flash of light from the other end of the bay.

"Hold," said Corbin.

"That was a muzzle flash," said Nelson.

Three more flashes came in rapid succession.

"And that was three more," I said.

"Nikolai, come with me," said Corbin. "We'll have a look, see if they're friend or foe. The rest of you, wait here until I call."

I nodded, realized that was a waste of effort, and said "Roger" instead. I walked forward to join Corbin. He had his K7 at the ready, so I drew the machine pistol and keyed the safety off. It was clumsy in the suit, but the gauntlets were close-fitting enough that I could get my finger inside the trigger guard, and that was the important part.

We moved forward as quietly as we could. Well, not quietly, since we were in a vacuum. But gently. Air or not, the vibrations of our footsteps would carry through the deck plates. Those commandos had all kinds of sensors in their helmets, so they would probably see us coming no matter what we did.

Based on the flashes we'd seen, I had the impression that something else held the entirety of their attention at the moment, though.

We reached the archway that led from cargo bay seven to cargo bay five. It was huge, large enough for two of the cargo drones to fly through simultaneously while carrying a full-sized shipping container. Corbin crouched at the starboard edge of the arch, and I ducked next to him, peering into the bay.

There I saw the signs of a battle. Several stacks of containers had been knocked into disorderly heaps, and one of them had split open, spilling grain everywhere. About a dozen yards away lay one of the Social Party commandos, sprawled in an untidy heap… and it looked as if the top half of his helmet and most of his head was missing. The contents of his head were leaking into a puddle around the shattered helmet.

I was suddenly glad I couldn't smell anything but recycled air.

Something huge darted overhead, and I looked up to see the missing cargo drone flying past. The antigrav units on its underside were sputtering, and bullet holes riddled its entire structure. The thing had taken what looked like dozens of rounds of high-caliber bullets, but it was still flying, albeit with an alarming wobble. As I watched, the drone banked left, releasing a large cargo crate of equipment.

It crashed to the deck and shattered in silence, though the impact made my bones vibrate within my suit. As the crate shattered, I saw a half-dozen commandos take cover, ducking behind one of the overturned shipping containers. It looked as if they had been trying to fight their way to the starboard side of the bay, to the access airlocks to the ship proper.

I blinked, astonished, as I realized where they were heading. To the control office for the cargo bay itself. Someone was there and they were using the massive drone as a weapon!

Every cargo bay had its own control office, where a tech monitored the operation of the drones and the other cargo handling systems. In theory, everything was controlled automatically from the bridge. In practice, when moving tens of thousands of tons of cargo, something always went wrong, so it was a good idea to have a living man down in the cargo office, keeping an eye on the machinery. It was cheaper to pay someone to do it than to lose ten thousand tons of cargo because two of the drones decided to fly into each other. The office itself was a small room with a window overlooking the bay, about halfway up the wall, a set of metal stairs climbing to it. Hundreds of bullet holes marked the wall and slashed the transparent metal of the window.

In the window I saw Arthur Rodriguez hunched over a console, wearing an orange pressure suit. He looked back and forth between the console and the damaged window, typing furiously. As far as I could tell, he was unhurt, although to judge from the amount of damage to the office airlock and window, he wasn't going to stay that way for long.

"Clever kid," said Corbin. "He weaponized the cargo drones. He's been keeping the commandos tied up down here all by himself! Nelson! Murdock! Bring up the rest of the men, fast and quiet. There are six commandos down here, and six more dead ones. That's at least a quarter of Ducarti's entire force, and if we move fast we have a chance to take them all out now."

Nelson and Murdock acknowledged, and I watched as the commandos sent another volley of fire at the office. The cargo drone swept before the wall, soaking up some of the fire, and released a crate of loading equipment from one of its claws. The crate struck the deck and bounced, again forcing the commandos to scatter and take cover.

"Right," I said. "How are we going to take them out?"

"I'll keep an eye on them," said Corbin. "See if you can raise Rodriguez."

"Roger that," I said. Corbin started giving orders over the suits' radio channel. I switched channels. "Arthur?" I got nothing but static. I tried to remember the channel for the cargo bays, failed, and started cycling. "Arthur? Arthur? This is Nikolai Rovio. Arthur, talk to me. Arthur?"

"Wait!" Arthur's voice hissed over the helmet speakers. "Wait! This is Rodriguez. Is someone there?" I heard a metallic thumping over the speakers, and realized it was the sound of bullets slamming into the wall of the cargo office.

"It's Nikolai," I said, watching Arthur peer out of the office window. "We're here to get you out. No! Don't look! The commandos don't know we're here yet." I glanced over my shoulder and saw Murdock and Nelson and the others come up, weapons ready. The cargo drone swept in front of the office again, and the commandos ducked for cover, though this time Arthur didn't drop anything on them. I recognized one of his favorite tactics from *Gunno-Tatakai*—keep the enemy guessing by being unpredictable.

So games had real practical applications! I suddenly felt my entire childhood had been justified.

"How are you still alive?" said Arthur. "I thought they had taken over the whole ship."

"They have," I said. "Well, sort of."

"Nikolai!" said Corbin, overriding my suit's radio settings. "Can you raise him or not?"

"Uh, yeah," I said. "I got him. We were just talking. Hang on." I fumbled back to Arthur's channel. "Arthur! Switch to channel four. My uncle's got an idea."

Static crackled inside my helmet, and then Arthur's voice came on. "This is Rodriguez."

"Rodriguez!" said Corbin. "Good to see that you're still alive. Nice work with the drones."

"Hey Rovio," said Arthur. "I'm keeping them off me for now. Do you know what is going on and who is trying to kill us?"

"The captain turned out to be a secret Social and he surrendered the ship to some Social Party raiders," said Corbin. "So we're going to take it back from them. How are you controlling that cargo drone, anyway? The captain locked us out of the ship's systems."

The drone swept before the office once more, soaking up another volley of gunfire. "My damage control assignment was in here. I figured that while I was waiting, I could do some tests. That idiot Murdock said my code was unoptimized–"

"Still alive here," said Murdock. "Good to see you too, Rodriguez."

"Oh. Hey. Likewise," said Arthur. "Anyway, I came down here to recompile and run some test routines while I was waiting for any sign we were taking damage. I saw the central systems were locking up, and I was worried that blockade runner was hacking us. So I cut off the cargo office's computer from the rest of the network. Then those pirates showed up and demanded I surrender. I figured that was a bad idea."

"So you started dropping crates on them," said Corbin. "You got six. Well done."

"I may have broken a few safety protocols and procedures," said Arthur.

"All of them," confirmed Nelson, with approval in his voice.

"We need to get you out of there," said Corbin, "and we might need that computer. Here's what we're going to do. Murdock, Nelson. Get the others deployed in the archway. Nikolai, stay where you are. Make sure you have clear lines of sight, and choose your targets. I want at least one gun on every commando."

"Got it," said Nelson, and he began barking instructions over the channel.

"Rodriguez," said Corbin. "Can you have the drone to come low over the deck, like, say, a meter? Have it swoop down towards the commandos, and then head for the ceiling?"

"Yeah," said Arthur. I saw him type something on his console. "Yeah, I think so. The antigravs are working well enough for that."

"Good," said Corbin. "Get that going. Nelson! The commandos are going to hit the deck when the drone dives toward them. When they do, we'll open fire."

"We're just going to shoot them all in the back?" said Nelson.

"Exactly," said my uncle. "If it troubles your conscience, try to remember they were going to kill everyone on the ship. Rodriguez, you ready yet?"

"Just a second," said Arthur. The commandos sent another volley of fire at the office window, and I saw Arthur duck under the console for a moment. "Hang on… yeah. It'll execute as soon as I hit the button. Tell me when."

"Do it on three," ordered Corbin. "Everyone, as soon as the commandos take cover, start shooting. Shoot to kill, and don't skimp on the ammo or the charges. We can get more from their dead bodies. Rodriguez?"

"Standby!" said Arthur, ducking to avoid a burst of concentrated fire. The window to the office absorbed the volley, but the transparent metal was bending backwards out of its frame. If one of those Socials had the bright idea of throwing a grenade through the damaged window, it was over. "All right! Three!"

He hit something on the console and ducked.

The cargo drone spun back into sight, all its arms and manipulators in motion, and it plummeted towards the deck. Some of the commandos opened fire, but the drone continued its rapid descent, and the rear antigravs pulsed, tilting the drone's nose towards the crouching commandos. For a moment it looked as if the big machine had lost control and was about to crash into the deck at full speed.

The commandos threw themselves down, ducking behind the damaged shipping containers and other debris left over from the fight. I could hardly blame them. Even from my vantage point, it looked terrifying and it wasn't about to land on my head.

But they were now in the worst possible position to deal with an attack of prepared gunmen from the rear.

"Open up!" said Corbin.

I raised my machine pistol in both hands and started shooting. The thing had a nasty recoil, but my gauntlets helped me keep my grip. I aimed for the head of the nearest commando, but I hit him in the lower back instead. The bullet punched through his armor and his torso, and I saw blood spatter across the deck beneath him. Around me the others had also opened fire, and a hail of bullets and invisible laser blasts slashed through the vacuum of cargo bay seven.

The commandos didn't have a chance. Two of them lived long enough to turn, and one of them even got off a burst from his K7, but it came nowhere near any of us. A second, equally furious volley cut them down, and they joined their motionless comrades on the floor.

I gripped my gun, breathing hard, but it was over. All the commandos were down.

"Anyone hit?" said Corbin. "Everyone acknowledge now."

One by one we checked in.

"Good work, everybody," Corbin praised us. "Nelson, search the dead. We'll need all the weapons we can carry. Do it quickly. I want to be on our way to the bridge in another five minutes. Murdock, take the techs and keep watch. I don't want to be surprised like our dead friends here. Rodriguez, it's safe. You can come out now."

"Rovio, I'm stuck," said Arthur. "The bullets messed up the airlock. I need someone to release it manually from the outside."

"Nikolai, do it," said Corbin. "Rodriguez, were you using the office's portable terminal?"

"Yeah."

"Bring it with you," said Corbin. "A working computer's going to be real useful soon."

"I'm on it," I said, switching my pistol's safety back on and shoving it back into the holster. I got it in on the third try. Funny that it was easier to shoot the thing than to holster it while wearing pressure suit gauntlets.

I scrambled up the metal stairs to the cargo office, taking care to keep my balance. There were a lot of metal fragments on the stairs, bullets deformed from ricocheting off the wall, along with pieces of the cargo drone's outer casing. The drone had taken a beating, but it was still flying. Whatever Starways had paid for the thing had been well worth the investment.

I reached the top of the stairs, and saw Arthur through the damaged window. I also saw the displays on the office's main console. Like all the displays in the engineering room or the bridge, they read SYSTEM LOCKED, but Arthur had a laptop-sized portal terminal on the desk, a maze of wires coming off the back. Usually drone operators had five or six full-sized displays, but he had been making the cargo drone dance with a little 14-inch screen.

I knocked on the window, realized that was stupid, and then activated my suit's radio. "Arthur?"

"Nikolai?" said Arthur. "You're there?"

"Who else?" I said. "Ready?"

"Hang on," he said, mashing his fingers against the laptop's keyboard. Below the drone swerved, and then flew back up to the ceiling, rotating itself into one of the cradles. "Just wanted to put that thing on standby. I dumped so many overrides into its task queue that I don't want it to go berserk and start loading us into shipping containers or something."

"That would be a bad end to the day," I said, examining the door controls. The commandos had shot it up pretty badly, but the manual release was still intact. "I'm going to try opening the door now… there!"

The door shuddered open. Had there been any air in the bay, it would have made a horrible squealing noise, so it was just as well we were in vacuum. The door managed to get about two-thirds of the way open before it gave up, so I squeezed through it and into the cargo office.

"Ready yet?" I said. "Corbin wants to move out. We're going to hit the bridge."

"Just about," said Arthur, stuffing the laptop and its attendant cables into a bag. It looked like he had spare charges in there as well. It would not be amusing if we finally found a working computer only for the power to run out on us. He slung over the bag over his shoulder. "Okay. I'm ready."

"Great," I said. "Let's go."

"I'm just glad I get to leave at all," said Arthur as I turned towards the door. "I thought I was going to die in here like a drone with a faulty… oh, wait!"

"What is it?" I said, turning, my hand dropping to my holstered gun.

"Almost forgot," said Arthur, picking up a flat black portable drive from the console. A piece of silver cargo tape had been affixed to the side, marked with the handwritten letters GT. "I'm out of pockets. Can you take that?"

"Yeah, sure," I said, slipping the drive into a pocket of my suit. "What is it? Drone code?"

"Our savegames," said Arthur.

I blinked several times.

"If we live through this," I said, "we're totally going to finish the main campaign."

"Nikolai! Arthur!" said Corbin, his voice cutting into my helmet speakers. "Hurry up!"

"On our way," I said. "Come on!"

We squeezed through the door and scrambled down the stairs. The others were ready, and bore considerably more weapons after looting the corpses. One of the men stepped forward, and I saw my uncle's face behind the helmet's faceplate.

"Rodriguez, great work," said Corbin. "You may have saved the ship."

"What's happening, sir?" said Arthur. "These guys with guns. Pirates?"

"Not exactly," said Corbin. "Nikolai can fill you in. We're heading to the bridge. Nelson?"

"Better arm yourself, son," said Nelson, handing Arthur a folded gun belt with a holstered burst laser pistol. "There was fighting behind us, and there's going to be fighting ahead of us."

"Fantastic," said Arthur, taking the belt.

"Good work with the drone, Rodriguez," said Murdock.

"Thanks. I wish we could take it with us," said Arthur. "I thought you were dead, Murdock."

"He's too cranky to die," I said.

"Everyone, shut up," ordered Corbin. "We're moving out. I'm on point. Nelson, Nikolai, keep an eye on the back."

Chapter 7

Modern Security Systems

We passed through the remaining port-side cargo bays without encountering any more trouble. Corbin hot-wired the airlock, and we filed into the gloomy maintenance walkways. They were pressurized, so we could take off our helmets and our gauntlets, though Corbin and Nelson insisted we keep our suits on in the event of a hull breach. Fortunately, the suits' belts had a magnetic grip for the helmets, which in turn made a handy bucket for holding the gauntlets.

"Now what?" said Murdock.

"We retake the bridge, rescue Hawkins, and capture the captain," said Corbin.

"And then shut down the resonance in the hypermatter reactor," said Arthur. I had filled him in our adventures, and while he seemed unfazed by the prospect of getting shot to death, the thought of the ship blowing up troubled him far more. He always did like machines better than people.

"That's the plan," said Corbin.

"I suggest we split up," said Nelson.

"Why?" said Murdock.

"Once we get to the bridge one team can go through the main blast doors, and the other can go through the access hatch to the maintenance walkways. If we catch the commandos in a crossfire, our chances of success will improve considerably."

"Agreed," said Corbin, "but we'll have to split up long before we get to the bridge, if I remember right…"

"Junction 17," I said.

They all looked at me.

"That's where the maintenance walkways split up," I said. "One goes to the bridge, the other goes to the dorsal corridor. If we split up, that's the best place to do it."

Corbin looked at Arthur, who nodded, fished his laptop out of the bag, and started pulling up a map of the ship. All our personal devices had been disabled when Williams had locked the computer, so we couldn't just check with them.

"He's right," said Arthur.

"Of course I'm right," I said. "I had to memorize the ship's schematic for one of my certification tests."

"Good," said Corbin. "We'll do it there."

"And if we run into more of Ducarti's men?" said Murdock.

"We might not," said Corbin. "That troop carrier could only hold thirty or forty, which means he's lost anywhere from twenty-five to forty percent of his men by now, especially after that last fight. That's not a lot of men to hold a ship this size, especially since he'll need to focus on the bridge and the engineering sections."

"He probably sent some men to the engineering room," said Nelson, "after you taunted him over the radio like that."

"That," I said, "and he needs the CPU for the hypermatter regulator before the ship blows up."

"Exactly," said Corbin. "The *Rusalka's* a big ship, and he won't have enough men to crawl over every inch looking for us. Especially if any other of the crew put up a fight. He'll probably be on the bridge to keep an eye on Williams and to oversee his men. If we strike hard and fast, we might be able to overwhelm his men and seize control of the bridge."

We stood in silence for a moment.

"Well," said Murdock finally. "It's not as if I have a better idea."

"That's the spirit," said Corbin.

"We're all in single file here, and those K7s are powerful. One good burst would kill us all. We ought to send someone ahead to scout around the corners, make sure we don't walk into an ambush."

"Excellent suggestion, Rovio" said Corbin. "Lead on."

Right then and there I learned a universal truth—if you point out a problem, you're the one who gets to fix it. So I sighed, slipped off the safety on my machine pistol, and took the lead.

"Nelson, go with him," said Corbin. "Back him up."

"All right," agreed Nelson. At Arthur's suggestion, we took a moment to remove the radio modules from our helmets and clip them to our ears. Since the ship's computer was still locked, our phones wouldn't work, but the helmet's radio modules would let us stay in touch when we split up.

We made our way through the narrow walkways. Nelson and I took the lead, proceeding forward to every junction, and summoning the others once the way was clear. We made good time, and began climbing up the ladders between decks, ascending to the dorsal level. As we passed the crew deck, I saw many familiar equipment nodes. Most of the life support machinery occupied the crew deck, and so I had spent a lot of time down here, fixing the endless things that could go wrong with carbon scrubbers and air filters and the waste recyclers.

So I was very familiar with the equipment in this area of the ship. That saved my life.

I peered around the corner, keeping my head low. Nelson said that most people didn't bother to look down, and rarely looked at things below their eye level. I didn't know if that was true or not, but it made sense. The maintenance walkway around the corner looked little different than the others. Bundles of cables hung in racks along the walls, and beneath the metallic grillwork of the floor ran a dozen thick metal pipes, each of them marked with dire warnings. A dozen more pipes followed the ceiling, each of them labeled with the same warnings. I had once spent several days checking pipe integrity, because if coolant got into the air circulators, it would kill a lot of people, so I knew this particular length of walkway pretty well.

However, I did not remember a lump of black metal clinging to the ceiling about twenty yards down the corridor. It looked kind of like a big metal spider, but with a number of lumps upon its back. In fact, one of those lumps suddenly began rotating around rather quickly.

"Anything?" said Nelson, impatient. "What is—"

"Back!" I shouted, shoving him. Nelson barked a curse, and a dozen shouted questions came from the others.

Right about then, the thing clinging to the ceiling pipes opened fire.

I was already moving, which was the only reason I didn't get cut in half. I glimpsed the stuttering muzzle flash from the black spider-thing, and I heard the loud clang as bullets struck the wall and bounced off, accompanied by the flash of sparks as one of the shots chewed into a wiring box. Something hot and painful ripped along my left temple, pain shooting down my neck, and I fell backwards with a grunt as dizziness washed through me. I heard Corbin shouting orders, and then someone grabbed my arms and dragged me backwards. I blinked and looked up as Arthur and Nelson pulled me back.

"Man down!" barked Nelson.

"Wait," I said. "I'm all right!" I sat up, and another wave of dizziness went through me, but it passed. I felt something wet on my left temple and realized that I was bleeding. I lifted a hand to my temple and felt blood there, along with a nasty gash. Just one of the bullets had barely grazed me, and it felt as if I had been hit in the head with a thrown baseball.

If that bullet had hit my forehead, it would have exploded my head like a melon in vacuum.

"Take cover!" said Nelson, and we scrambled, pressing ourselves against the walls. It was an exercise in futility. Even with the wiring racks and pipes lining the walls, we were at least three-quarters exposed. Any competent marksman could kill half of us with as many shots. Or finish us all of with a single fragmentation grenade.

Yet strangely, no additional shots were fired.

"How many were there?" said Corbin, holding his K7.

I shook my head, which hurt. "No men. Some sort of robot or drone thing."

Nelson's grimace tightened. "I didn't get a good look at it."

"It was like a big metal spider," I said. "Hanging from the ceiling. It had some sort of turret on its back, and it spun around to point at us."

Corbin and Nelson looked at each other.

"Security drone," they said in unison.

"Socials must have brought some aboard when they took the ship," said Nelson.

"Makes sense," said Corbin. "Ducarti must have deployed them once he realized he was losing men."

"Should we be moving?" I asked my uncle. "If that thing comes around the corner, it could gun us all down without much trouble."

Corbin shook his head. "A security drone like that has very limited AI. It will sit there and defend its perimeter until Ducarti recalls it." He frowned at me. "You're bleeding. There should be a medical kit in that equipment locker, so get yourself cleaned up."

I nodded, slipped past the others, and opened up the equipment locker. It held the usual collection of emergency gear and tools in a maintenance walkway—a small medical kit, some emergency tools for dealing with hull breaches, pressure masks, a fire extinguisher, and so forth. There was a little plastic mirror in the door, and I flinched a little when I saw my reflection. The near-miss from the bullet had left a lot more blood that I expected. No wonder my head hurt so much. Between that and the stun grenade earlier… how long ago had that been? An hour and a half, maybe? It felt like months.

Anyway, given all the abuse my head had taken today, it was a miracle I was still conscious. If that security drone had slightly better aim, I would be dead, so I suppose it could have been worse. I rummaged through the medical kit, found a bottle of painkillers, and swallowed three tablets. There were also several self-sealing bandages, equipped with disinfectant, and I slapped one of them over the cut on my temple. That hurt, a lot, but I supposed that was better than dying of an infection in a week or so.

Though at the moment, living long enough to die of an infection would be a triumph of sorts.

I turned back as Nelson, Murdock, and Corbin argued about what to do.

"Maybe we can work up some kind of shield, shoot at the drone from behind it," said Murdock.

"I doubt that," said Nelson. He scooped up one of the deformed bullets from the deck. "These are high enough caliber that they'll rip through anything we can improvise into armor. We're lucky it didn't punch through the wall to reach the cargo bays, else we'd be in vacuum by now."

"So the stupid thing will just sit there and shoot anyone who comes at it?" said Murdock.

"Until it runs out of bullets," said Corbin. "Or grenades. Or power in its laser capacitators. Security drones sometimes have multiple armaments." He looked at Nelson. "Think we can take it out?"

"Probably not," said Nelson. "I don't think it was a large drone. Nikolai, you had a better look. How large was it?"

I frowned, wincing a little at the pain it sent through my head. A pity the medical kit didn't have anything stronger. "The size of a cat, maybe?"

"Half-inch of armor, at least," said Nelson. "We could take it down, but it will kill quite a few of us."

Corbin shook his head. "Not an option. We need everyone who can carry a gun when it comes time to storm the bridge."

"There are other ways to the bridge," said Arthur. "We could all circle back to the dorsal corridor and attack the blast doors."

"We have to hit the bridge in two directions at once," said Corbin. "Else we will be overwhelmed easily. All the commandos have K7s and armor."

"What about EVA?" said Nelson. "We have the suits. We could cross the hull and come in through one of the upper airlocks."

Corbin shook his head. "These suits are designed for the cargo bay, not for EVA along the hull. It would keep the radiation at bay for a few hours but one slip and you'll be gone. Maybe as a last resort."

That and the other ships would likely pick up movement outside the hull. They'd be looking for it.

"Well, we're wasting time," said Murdock. "That drone might have alerted Ducarti, and if he's got any men to spare they'll be on their way. We've got to make a decision now."

"Very well," said Corbin reluctantly.

"Wait!" I said. "I've got an idea."

I popped the little plastic mirror out of the door and grabbed a big wrench from the tool kit, the kind designed for securing airlock mounting bolts. I took a tube of breach foam, sprayed some on the end of the wrench, and slapped the mirror against it.

"What in space are you doing?" said Murdock.

"I think that drone was hanging from something useful," I said. "I need another look at it without getting my head shot off." I stopped before the corner, dropped down the floor, and pressed myself flat.

Then, inch by inch, I stuck the wrench and the mirror out around the corner.

Any moment I expected the wrench to get shot out of my hand, but the trick worked. Evidently the drone's sensors couldn't lock onto something so small, or maybe the thing just wasn't looking down. I angled the wrench back and forth, trying to spot the drone, and at last I saw it hanging from the ceiling conduits, looking like a big black spider bristling with antennae.

And a double-barreled automatic gun.

Nelson grunted as he squatted next to me, peering into the mirror. "Nasty thing. Mark VII perimeter defense drone."

"But we're in luck," said Corbin. "The Mark VII drones are autonomous, not networked. It will sit here until Ducarti specifically recalls it."

"Which means it hasn't phoned home," I said.

"Nope," said Nelson.

"Still don't know how we're going to get around the thing," said Murdock. "Got any ideas about that?"

"Actually," I said, tilting the mirror a little more. "I might. Look at where the drone is hanging."

"A bunch of pipes?" said Murdock. "So what?"

"Not any pipes. Hot water pipes for the heating and cooling system. That goes to one of the pumps... ah, pump 47B, if I remember correctly."

"He's right," said Corbin.

"If we shut the pump's valves and run the motor at maximum," I said, "the pump will rupture. In a big way. That would throw the drone off and we could disable it if we move fast."

"And how are we going to do that?" said Murdock. "We'd need computer access to the pump."

"We do," I said, retracting my improvised mirror. Then I jerked my thumb at Arthur. "Fortunately, he thought to bring a computer along." I got up, found a junction box in the bundles of wires along the wall, and pried it open. Inside waited an array of ports for local computer access. "We can plug in here."

Murdock frowned. "But if Rodriguez connects to the network, the central system will enforce the lockout."

"Not if he only talks to the pump," I said.

Corbin nodded. "Those ports are local access only. We can talk to the pump, and maybe a few other devices nearby."

Murdock gave him a sour look, but gestured at the junction box. Arthur handed me a data cable, and I connected it to the back of the laptop and plugged it into the appropriate port. The laptop's screen flashed, and white text started to scroll across the black screen.

"Right," said Corbin. "Rodriguez, hold that open for me. Nelson, Murdock. Get ready to jump around the corner and take that thing out." Nelson snapped a command to the other techs. "Wait until I give the word, but the right time will probably be obvious. Remember, you'll only have a few seconds before the drone rights itself, so don't dawdle."

The screen flashed again, and the text-based interface for pump 47B appeared on the display. "Well, Nikolai, what do you think?"

"Maximum water pressure, maximum water temperature, and zero outflow?" I said, recalling the list of things the manual had said to never, ever do with a water pump.

"That should do it," said Corbin, entering a string of commands into the laptop. "Nelson, Murdock. After I enter the command, we should have about… let me see."

I did some math in my head. "Nineteen seconds."

"Nineteen seconds before the pump explodes," Corbin confirmed, as he turned off the last safety and entering the administrative override mode. "Be ready. I'm entering the command… now."

He hit the enter key.

Nothing happened at first. About five seconds later I heard a faint humming sound from around the corner. The status messages scrolling on the laptop screen went from yellow, to orange, and then to red, and then to red in all capital letters. The humming noise grew louder and became a loud screeching sound.

That was followed by a watery explosion, shockingly loud in the confined space, followed by the gush of liquid and the hiss of steam.

"Now!" shouted Corbin, but Murdock and Nelson and two of the techs were already moving. They swung around the corner, leveled their weapons, and opened fire in a volley of bullets and laser bursts. I watched them with my heart pounding, half-expecting to see a burst of fire cut them down, but then Nelson stopped shooting, and the others followed suit.

"Drone down," announced the chief with satisfaction.

"Good," said Corbin, closing the laptop and handing it back to Arthur, who secured it in his case. "Let's move out. Watch your footing. It'll be slippery."

We went around the corner. The grillwork on the deck was gleaming with water from the ruptured pump, steam rising from the pipes, and I felt the wet, hot air like a slap in the face. The security drone lay on its back below the damaged pump, smoke rising from the craters blasted into its side. I looked at the pump and winced, imagining how much work it would take to pull it out of the ceiling, repair the damaged housing, remount the stripped pump engine, and then reinstall the entire thing. It was exactly the kind of tedious job Corbin would farm out to an apprentice.

I laughed at myself. If we lived through this mess, I would happily remount every single pump on the ship.

Murdock and I took point again, and we checked every corner and blind spot, watching for more security drones. We found two more clinging to the walls and ceilings, guns ready for any trespassers, but since we were ready for them we did not blunder into the trap. We took out one by blowing another pump, and Corbin destroyed the second with a well-placed grenade that knocked off the wall and permitted Nelson to put five rounds through its innards.

At last we reached the ship's top deck, and came to junction 17, not far from where Murdock and I had killed that first Social Party commando.

"All right," said Corbin. "This is how we'll play it. Nelson, go with Rodriguez to the main blast doors, and take two of the techs. Nikolai, Murdock, and the other techs will accompany me on the maintenance walkways to the bridge. Use the computer to open the bridge blast doors. When you do, signal us." He tapped the radio module clipped to his ear. "We'll come in through the access panel and attack at the same time. Between our two groups, we'll hopefully catch the Social Party commandos in a crossfire, and we can free Hawkins and take control of the ship."

"And the captain?" said Murdock.

"Take him alive if possible," said Corbin. "Hawkins can unlock the primary systems, but we'll need Williams to unlock the weapons. If you encounter Ducarti, kill him on sight. The man is too dangerous to leave alive."

Ever since the explosion on New Chicago, I had fantasized about taking vengeance upon Alesander Ducarti. I had also known it would never happen. The Thousand Worlds were a big place, and I probably would never see Ducarti again.

Now I might have the chance to kill him myself.

I didn't know how to feel about that. I did know that I wouldn't hesitate in the slightest to shoot him. I could sort out how I felt about it later.

"Radio check," said Corbin. We took a moment to make sure our radio modules were synchronized and functioning properly. "Good hunting, everyone. Stay calm and keep your heads down."

"You, too," said Nelson, checking something on his K7. "All right. Rodriguez, you two, come with me" Nelson head down the maintenance walkway, followed by Arthur and two of the techs, all holding their weapons ready.

"Follow me," said Corbin. We went in the other direction, came to an access ladder, and climbed it to the next deck. We found ourselves in the maintenance walkway running next to the dorsal corridor and the rooms on the top level of the ship—the bridge, the observation lounge, the computer room, the communications room, and the other control areas. I half-expected to find another set of security drones waiting for us, but the walkway was empty. I realized that Ducarti had thought to trap us in the cargo bays, and had arranged his drones accordingly. That meant there was likely an ambush of his men awaiting us in the main corridors outside of the cargo bays.

An ambush that we had eluded entirely.

"All right," said Corbin. "From this point on, keep quiet and speak only when necessary. You know how sound carries in these walkways." When working on the bridge in the past, I had heard all manner of clanks and clanging coming from the maintenance walkways. Corbin tapped his earpiece. "Nelson?"

Nelson's voice crackled over the little speaker. "We've reached the dorsal corridor. So far it's clear. I think most of the Socials are on the crew deck, holding the crew captive. I expect Ducarti's next play will be to start shooting hostages until we surrender."

"He might be up to something else," I said. "A misdirection. On New Chicago he made that big show about sending a petition to the government, but that was just a ruse to get his bomb close enough to the building. Maybe he's doing something like that now."

"Maybe," said Murdock, "but he can't do anything clever with a bullet through his head."

"If he's smart he's already run for the sublight ship," said Corbin. "Let's hope he's not smart. Nelson, we're almost to the access panel. Have Rodriguez override the door. Tell us when you go through. We'll break out and hit them from behind."

"Be quick about it, Rovio," said Nelson. "We won't have any cover in the corridor."

"I know," said Corbin. "We'll get the panel open as fast as we can, but we'll have to stay quiet from now on. Any sounds we make will be audible on the bridge."

"Roger," said Nelson. "We'll keep you updated. Rodriguez, get started on the locks. The rest of you, cover the blast doors. If anyone come out, shoot to kill."

A murmur of acknowledgments came over the radio, and Corbin lifted his finger to his lips. I nodded, as did Murdock and the other men. We filed in silence down the walkway, coming to an access panel at the end.

On the other side of the panel was the bridge, and God knew how many Social Party commandos. Maybe even Ducarti himself and his traitorous pet, Captain Williams.

Corbin pressed his ear to the panel for a moment, and I followed suit. I heard a faint murmur of conversation from the other side, but I couldn't discern any of the words. Corbin tapped one of the fasteners holding the panel in place, and I nodded, holstered my machine pistol, and produced my multitool. I started working through the fasteners on the bottom of the panel, while Corbin went to work on the top.

"Rodriguez," crackled Nelson's voice inside my helmet. "How's it coming?"

"Two more," said Arthur. "Uh… looks like the blast door has six deadbolts. Have to release them all manually. Okay, that's five. Just one more."

I popped off the last fastener and straightened up. Corbin gripped one side of the panel, and I took the other. Murdock stepped back, switched his K7 to single-shot mode, and pointed the weapon at the panel. The other two techs took up position behind him, their lasers ready.

"All right," said Arthur. "As soon as I release the last bolt, the doors should open automatically. Ready?"

"Ready," said Nelson. "Do it."

"Here goes," said Arthur.

For an moment, nothing happened. Then I heard a series of dull thumps vibrating through the grillwork beneath my boots, followed by the low whine of releasing hydraulics. A man's voice rose in a question, and then another.

The roar of gunfire filled my ears; I heard it through the access panel as well as through someone's live mike.

"Now!" said Corbin. We heaved, pulling the access panel from its mounting, and dropped it. I caught a glimpse of the bridge, saw a dozen crewmen on their knees with their hands behind their heads, and several commandos in dark armor hurrying towards the blast doors to the dorsal corridor.

Five of them. Maybe six. We were outgunned.

But once more, we had the advantage of surprise and position.

Murdock jumped through the opened panel, leveled his rifle, and started shooting. He hit one of the commandos through the head, and plugged a second in the shoulder before they realized that something had gone wrong. Then he threw himself through the hatch and into the bridge, hitting the ground and rolling. The return fire ripped into one of the consoles, but missed Murdock entirely. The commandos had their whole attention on him and on the dorsal corridor, and I heard the crack of bullets and the whine of burst lasers coming through the opened blast doors.

That gave me and Corbin and the other techs a perfect opportunity to attack.

I had yanked my pistol from its holster as Murdock charged, flipping off the safety. Corbin leaned around the left side of the hatch, K7 raised, while I went on the right. There were still six commandos standing in the bridge, with two motionless upon the deck. Hawkins was shouting something, and I saw the crew members rolling and trying to take cover from the gunfight. I also saw that their wrists had been bound, so they wouldn't be of any use at the moment.

One of the commandos facing the dorsal corridor reached for his belt and the row of grenades hanging there. That seemed like it a problem, so I aimed at him and started pulling the trigger. Murdock had gotten his first commando through the head. I wasn't nearly as good of a shot, but I did hit my target in the hip. I don't know if the round penetrated his armor or not, but it made him forget about his grenade. He started to turn in my direction, and I adjusted my aim for the center of his mass and squeezed the trigger three more times. I think I hit him all three times, because he slammed back against the side of the blast door and collapsed to the deck.

Corbin was loosing short, sharp bursts of full auto from his K7, aiming the weapon with expert skill. One of the commandos started to line up on him, and Corbin's next burst exploded the commando's helmet in a spray of twisted metal and shattered ceramic and blood. That took some of the pressure off Murdock, who popped over his console and squeezed off a few shots. Another commando shot at the access hatch, and I flinched back as the bullets pinged off the metal. Murdock hit the commando in the knee, and both Corbin and I fired at once. That commando staggered back, dropping his weapon, and collapsed to the deck.

The silence that followed was the most shocking thing I had ever heard. Or didn't hear. Or something. God, I don't think the firefight lasted more than thirty seconds, but it had felt like hours.

"Nelson!" called Corbin. "Report!"

Nelson stepped into the bridge, smoke rising from the barrel of his K7. "We're clear, Rovio. No KIA. One of the techs took a slug to the forearm but he shouldn't bleed out."

"We're clear here," said Corbin. He stepped into the bridge, and the rest of us followed him as Murdock got to his feet. "No sign of Ducarti? Or Williams?"

"None," said Nelson. "But at least we found the XO."

"They left," said Hawkins, and everyone looked at the XO, who had pushed himself to his feet. "Ducarti had four more men with him, and he and the captain took off in a hurry. I think they were going to the engineering room."

"Nikolai," said Corbin. "Start cutting them loose. We'll need every man we have who can carry a gun."

I nodded, produced my multitool, and got to work.

"Why?" said Hawkins as he massaged his newly freed wrists. "What do you think he's doing now? I think he might have lost at least half of his men."

"I think," said Corbin, "he's going to try and eject our hypermatter reactor."

Hawkins frowned. "But you entangled our reactor with his."

"I did," said Corbin. "Ejecting the reactor will cause it to destabilize and explode. But if the *Vanguard* ejects its reactor at the same time, the blockade runner will remain functional. The *Vanguard* will have its weapons online, and we won't, so it can blast us to pieces."

I started cutting through the restraints as fast as I could manage.

Chapter 8

Emergency Safety Procedures

I cut the last of the restraints, and the final crewer got to his feet, groaning and flexing his swollen hands. Hawkins rushed over to the XO's station and began typing, entering his codes to unlock the ship's systems and restore its core functions. One by one, consoles came to life around the bridge, the displays flashing with numbers and letters, and the crewmen hurried to their seats.

Almost all of the screens were displaying various warnings and system errors.

One screen in particular displayed an ominous warning. According to the computer, we had somewhere between five hours and nineteen minutes and seven hours and forty-seven minutes until the hypermatter reactor destabilized and blew up the *Rusalka*. Due to the inherent quantum uncertainty involved in hypermatter reactions, the computer couldn't predict the exact time the entangled reactors would blow up and destroy both the hyper-locked ships, but if Corbin didn't restore the regulator within the next six hours or so, we were all going to die.

"Did he say anything useful?" said Corbin. "Either him or the captain?"

"No," said Hawkins. He didn't seem to mind that Corbin had taken charge. I was pretty sure that Corbin had more combat experience than Hawkins. I wondered if Hawkins had known that Corbin had been part of Coalition intelligence, or that the cargo held a secret list of Social Party agents, and decided that it didn't matter just now.

"What did they talk about?" said Corbin.

"They kept calling in different crew members to question them about the grain," said Hawkins. "They were convinced that list Ducarti wanted was encoded in the grain, can you believe that?"

"It is," said Corbin.

"You might have mentioned that," said Hawkins with a scowl. I guess he didn't know.

"I've been saying that for hours," said Murdock from another console.

"Yes, and I heard you the first time," said Corbin, a little sharply. "We all thought Williams was crooked. You never suspected he had gone over to the revolutionaries and neither did I." He shook his head. "That's why we arranged for the grain to ship aboard the *Rusalka*. None of the Social Party privateers have the firepower to take a ship this size"

"That's why they suborned the captain," said Hawkins, stooping over another console and entering a string of commands.

"You see the problem," said Corbin. "Do we have any of the sensor operators here?"

"No," said Hawkins. "I've only seen about thirty of the crew. I'm hoping that Ducarti didn't kill them all, that they're holed up in the galley or crew quarters."

"Let's find out," said Corbin. "See if you can unlock the internal sensor systems. Nikolai! Get on the sensor console. Full interior scan, focusing on life signs and weapon traces."

I nodded and dropped into the seat at the sensor console. The displays still read SYSTEM LOCKED, but after a moment they flashed and reset. I started typing and flipping the switches. The *Rusalka* had a full suite of exterior sensor: radar, lidar, infrared, hyperspace distortion, neutrino-V and neutrino-H. The interior sensors weren't nearly so elaborate. But it did have infrared detectors for picking up body heat, along with a few other sensors designed to pick up weapons traces. I keyed for an internal scan, and seeing that the computer still had a lot of processing power available since so many primary systems were locked, I instructed it to do a full exterior scan next, since I figured Corbin would want to know what was going on outside of the ship.

A moment later the numbers flashed across the display, and a diagram of the *Rusalka's* crew areas appeared, dotted with red splotches to represent heat signatures.

"What do we have?" said Corbin.

"The ship counts one hundred and twenty-one of the crew are still alive."

Hawkins raised his eyebrows. "We lost only nine? I thought Ducarti would start shooting people right and left."

"If he's going to blow up the ship, why go to the trouble?" said Corbin. "Nikolai. Zoom in there." I tapped some keys, and another list appeared on the display. "It looks like… only fifteen commandos are left."

"Fifteen?" I said, astonished. "Only fifteen? That troop ship of his could have held forty."

"Maybe he didn't have the full forty aboard," said Corbin. "I suspect he expected even less resistance than he actually faced. Williams likely promised more than he could deliver."

"Still," I said, a little surprised. "Only fifteen left? It's hard to believe that he brought so few."

"Not really," said Corbin. "Ducarti's not a soldier or a pirate. He's a speechmaker and a terrorist. Convincing people to kill themselves for the Social Party, or tricking them into it, that plays to his strengths. Seizing a ship is something else entirely. He's a novice at this, and probably assumed that Williams locking down the ship would neutralize all resistance."

"I had to take a crowbar to an arms locker," said Nelson.

"Murdock had some laser pistols in the computer room," I said.

"That's against regulation," said Nelson at once.

Murdock shrugged from where he was working at one of the computer consoles. "Staying alive is its own regulation."

"Plus, he couldn't have foreseen Rodriguez using a cargo drone like that," said Corbin, "or how that would arm us. No, he's improvising now. That's good. Improvising men make mistakes, which means we have about a fifty-fifty chance of getting out of this alive since he wasn't smart enough to cut his losses and run."

"It looks like there are only about five commandos guarding the crew decks," said Hawkins, pointing at one of my displays. To judge from the mass of infrared signatures, he was right.

"Five men to guard nearly ninety seems risky," I said.

Murdock grunted, walking to another console. "Not when those five have K7 automatics. No one wants to go first and be the dead hero."

"Good point," I said. We'd both gone to the airlock like sheep, after all.

"Where are the rest of them?" said Nelson.

"It looks like you're right. Ducarti, ten commandos, and Captain Williams are heading for the engineering room," I said. "Do you think they can do that ejection thing you mentioned?"

"I doubt it, unless they happened to have the right kind of processor aboard the *Vanguard*, he could stabilize our hypermatter reactor. They're probably just checking out my story; that's why he hasn't run for it. For all he knows, I was bluffing."

"All right," said Hawkins. "We have two priorities, then. First, to rescue the crew with as little loss of life as possible. Second, to stop Ducarti from disentangling the hypermatter regulator."

"Hey, if he can do it, that's not a problem," Murdock cut in. "If we don't, the ship blows up. You already bought us the time we needed."

"I suggest that our second priority should be to stop Ducarti from escaping on the troopship," said Corbin. "However that happens, whether through his death, neutralization, or surrender. I also suggest that our third priority ought to be to stabilize the hypermatter reactor as soon as possible."

I wondered if Hawkins realized how smoothly Corbin had taken charge. Or maybe he did and was grateful for the help. The XO wasn't a stupid man, after all.

"Agreed," said Hawkins. "Since he's not trying to escape yet, we should free the crew before they're all slaughtered. There are only five commandos on the crew deck. Can we storm the crew quarters?"

"Probably," said Nelson, "but losses will be high. They'll have set up fortified positions. Worse, they'll be able to take hostages, and if we don't take them out cleanly, we'll lose a lot of people."

"We have control of the life support systems again," said Corbin. "Perhaps we can put those to use."

"Pump gas into the crew deck, you mean?" said Hawkins. "Try to knock them out?"

"Something like that," said Corbin.

"Won't work," called Murdock. "All those commandos have gas masks built into their helmets, probably a nice little air filtration system. They can operate in hard vacuum, too. The men we killed in cargo bay seven didn't have any trouble operating there. We could pump the air out of the crew deck, or pump in anything else we wanted, and it wouldn't have any effect."

"Anything we could pump into the deck that would penetrate those gas masks," said Hawkins, "would also kill the entire crew well before it harmed the commandos. If we could just evacuate the hostages first, that would…"

I blinked as an idea came to me.

"Wait," I said. Hawkins looked at me. "Sorry to interrupt, sir. But did you unlock the internal communications? And the door systems?"

Yeah," said Hawkins. "Those are all a subset of the communications system and life support control, and I unlocked those right away." He scowled. "Still can't access her weapons, though, which would solve a lot of problems."

"But we can control the doors," I said. "And the comms." I pointed at the internal sensor screen. "Most of the crew still have their receivers. We can send them a message, telling them to retreat into the maintenance walkways. All the commandos are in the corridors keeping guard. We'll seal every door on that deck, which will give the crew time to get away. By the time the commandos break through the doors, the crew will be gone, and then we can pump all the air out. They can't have more than an hour or two of air in their suits. They'll either surrender or asphyxiate."

For a moment no one said anything, and then Hawkins snorted.

"You know, Rovio," he said. "I always thought you were too clever for your own good. Sounds like he takes after you."

"Don't remind me," said Corbin. "There are a lot of ways this could go wrong, but I can't think of anything better. I say we do it."

"Very well," said Hawkins. "Were any of the environmental techs with you?"

"No," said Corbin. "Looks like they're all on the crew deck. Rodriguez!" Arthur hurried over, still carrying his laptop. "You hear all that?"

"Some of it," said Arthur, looking pretty nervous for a guy who'd single-handedly killed six armored commandos.

"You've got the most experience on the environmental systems, so take over," he said, pointing at the life support console.

"I'm a cargo specialist," said Arthur. "If I screw up, I could kill them all."

"Think of it as unloading human cargo," said Corbin.

"My point is that you have more experience with the enviro systems than I do," said Arthur.

"This is why we cross-train," said Corbin. "I would do it, but I need to be elsewhere. I wouldn't ask you to do it unless I was certain you could manage it. You were cool under much worse pressure in the cargo bay. You can do this."

Arthur nodded, seeming to recover his confidence. But he had only been responsible for his own life in the cargo bay. He would have the lives of over one hundred men in his hands.

Yeah, I see how he could get nervous.

"Where are you going?" said Hawkins.

"With your permission, I will lead an attack to seize control of the engineering room," said Corbin. "We can't let Ducarti stabilize the reactor, and even if that is not his objective, we need to keep him occupied and prevent him from reaching the troopship."

"I should be the one to go," said Hawkins. "With Williams turned traitor, I'm in command of this ship."

"Which is exactly why you shouldn't go," said Corbin. "If I'm killed, someone will have to take charge, and someone needs to stay here on the bridge and coordinate now that we have communications back."

Hawkins hesitated, but not for long. "All right. That's your job, then. Go to the engineering section and take it back. Clear out the remaining Socials and stop whatever they're trying to do." He exhaled and shook his head. "And try to stop the hypermatter reactor from blowing up, will you? We need it to get home."

"Aye aye, Skipper," said Corbin.

"Take whoever you need with you," said Hawkins, standing a little taller, "and whatever weapons you want."

"Right," said Corbin. "Murdock, stay here with Rodriguez. Make sure everything goes well on the crew deck. Nelson, you're with me. Pick out fifteen men, and as many weapons as we can carry." Nelson nodded in his customarily unfazed manner and started choosing men, assigning them the weapons captured from the slain Social Party commandos. "Nikolai, you're with me."

"Me?" I said, surprised.

"You've kept your head in a firefight," said Corbin. "Twice now. Not many men can say that. I know I can count on you."

A surge of pride went through me. I was tired and sore, and my head and neck and back hurt from the battering they had taken. I really, really wanted to go lie down someplace and sleep for a month, and I desperately wished that I had never seen Alesander Ducarti ever again.

But I would not have traded that moment for anything.

"Yes, sir," I said.

Corbin smiled at me. "Get some reloads from Nelson."

My machine pistol was almost empty, but as it turned out, reloading it proved no great challenge. The commandos had been armed to the teeth, and we had taken enough weapons and ammunition to conquer a small colony, or at least a mid-sized space station. Now that the ship's systems were partially unlocked, our comms worked again, so Nelson distributed earpieces, pairing them to our devices and locking them into a private channel. Williams would be able to listen in, if he happened to think of it, but the encryption on the private channel would keep him from understanding any of it.

"All right, men, listen up," said Nelson. "We're going to go take back our engineering room from the Socials. Mr. Rovio has a plan. Corbin?"

"We've got the internal sensors and security grid back," said Corbin, "so we can at least see what's going on. Nikolai? Bring up the view from the engineering room, please."

I nodded, walked to the sensor console, and tapped some keys. The air over the bridge's main holographic projector flickered, and a hazy black-and-white image from the engineering room's security camera appeared. The *Rusalka's* internal sensors could pick up infrared, weapons traces, and radiation leaks, but for all that, the internal cameras were low-resolution, and there was only one camera in the engineering room. I supposed Starways had to cut costs somewhere. Nevertheless, in the hazy image, I could count eleven armored commandos standing guard over the consoles.

I couldn't see Ducarti or Williams anywhere. Though given how little of the engineering room the camera covered, that didn't mean anything.

"They've got a good defensive position," Nelson observed.

"Yes," said Corbin, "but they're all clustered in the engineering room. According to the internal sensors, none of them have gotten into the surrounding maintenance walkways, including the crawlway that runs over the top of the room. We'll send a man above to drop a few stun grenades into the engineering room. Once they're incapacitated, we'll storm the room."

Suddenly I realized why my uncle wanted me to come along. There were occasional downsides to being young and skinny.

"That should work," said Nelson. "So long as they don't spot the man infiltrating."

"We need to do it as soon as possible. The longer they're in the engineering room, the longer they have to make trouble. If we retake the engineering room and take them out, I can stabilize the hypermatter react and we all live to go home. Any objections?"

No one had any.

"XO," said Corbin. "How are things on the crew deck?"

"Murdock," said Hawkins.

Murdock stood next to Arthur, who sat at the life support control console, typing furiously. "I've gotten in touch with the men on the crew decks. They've taken cover, and we've sealed the doors. I don't think the Socials on the crew deck have realized it yet. Hopefully they won't figure out what we're doing until Rodriguez here has finished pumping all the air out of the corridors."

"You've still got the radio we took from the dead commando's helmet?" said Corbin.

"Right here," said Murdock. He glanced at the dead commandos, who had been unceremoniously dumped against the wall to keep them out of the way. "I know where we can get a few more, too."

"Keep an eye on them," said Corbin. "Once they realize what we've done, get in touch and offer them a chance to surrender. I don't want to risk them going berserk and blowing holes in the side of the ship. Give them good terms—we'll dump them on the first inhabitable planet we find and go on our way."

I frowned. "After everything they've done?"

Corbin shrugged. "Best to leave the enemy a chance to escape, if necessary."

"There's no way to escape from the engineering room," said Nelson.

"I know," said Corbin. "Which is why this will be a hard fight. It's time to move out. Nikolai..."

"Take the stun grenades?" I said.

He blinked in surprise, then nodded again. "You're the best man for the job. I'll need you to climb into the maintenance walkways above the engineering room and drop the grenades. Once they go off, we'll charge the room and attack.

With luck, we can clear them out without taking too many casualties."

"And Ducarti and the captain?" said Nelson.

"Take them alive if you can," said Corbin. "And if not well, they had their chance. It's time to go."

"I'll coordinate from here," said Hawkins. "Good luck." He turned back to Arthur's console.

"Let's move out," said Corbin.

One of the techs handed me a tool bag. It currently held no tools, but instead contained eight stun grenades the commandos had carried onto the *Rusalka*. I nodded my thanks, slung the bag's strap across my chest, checked the safety on my machine pistol and the ammunition on my belt, and followed the others from the bridge. The blast doors slid shut behind us with an ominous clang, which seemed like a bad omen. Still, if this went bad, at least Ducarti and his surviving troops would not be able to break back into the bridge to take control of the ship.

We walked down the corridor in silence. Far at the other end of the dorsal corridor, I saw the opened doors to the engineering room. I wondered why the commandos beyond them did not open fire. They had a clear shot all the way up the dorsal corridor. Nelson kept us moving along the walls, ready to take cover in the other doorways should the enemy open up. I felt sweat trickling down my back beneath my jumpsuit and vacuum suit. Why weren't the commandos in the engineering room opening fire? It would have been so easy to pin us down.

"Nikolai," said Corbin, pointing at the side of the corridor. We had reached the navigation observation lounge, the very place where I had followed Murdock into the maintenance walkways. Further down the corridor would be the airlocks where the troop transport and the *Vanguard* would have docked with the *Rusalka*. An idea occurred to me.

"Why don't we take over the *Vanguard*?" I said. "Or the troop ship? Either one would keep Ducarti from getting away and leaving the ships to blow."

"A good idea," said Corbin, "but it looks like the Socials sealed both doors behind them. Both are connected to the *Rusalka* with an airlock, and if we used the kind of equipment we'd need to cut through their blast doors, we would likely rip open the tunnels to vacuum. No, we'd best regain control of the *Rusalka* first, and then deal with the other ships."

"Okay," I said. "I'll head for the maintenance walkways now."

"Nikolai," said Corbin quietly. I paused, and he clapped me on the shoulder. "I'm not going to say that your mother and father would be proud of you, because we both know they would not approve of what you have done. But that, I think, is the highest praise I can give you."

I grinned. "Mom would have been furious." My smile faded. "But maybe if Sergei had known the truth about Ducarti, maybe that would have changed his mind."

"Maybe," said Corbin. "If nothing else, we can avenge them. Good luck, Niko."

"You too," I said, and I took a firm grip on the grenade bag before entering the observation lounge.

The panel where Murdock and I had fled earlier was still loose, and it was no trouble to pry it off and move it aside. I climbed into the narrow passage and started down it, the boots of my suit clanking against the metal grill floor. I would head up to the next level, to the crawlway that wedged between the outer and inner hulls. From there I would make my way to the platform above the engineering room.

"Nikolai?" crackled Corbin's voice in my ear.

"I hear you," I said, making my way along, the bag of stun grenades thumping against me with every step. I slipped my machine pistol out of its holster, checked the safety, and kept it ready in my right hand. "I'll send a text when I'm in position." I didn't dare speak once I was in the crawlspace over the engineering room. The sound might reach the ears of the commandos, and then they would need only to send a few volleys of bullets into the ceiling to deal with me.

"Go as fast as you can," said Corbin. "We're in position. I expect the commandos know we're here, and the longer we wait, the more likely it is Ducarti will decide to start something."

"Roger," I said, stopping at the base of a ladder cylinder. "I'm climbing into the crawlspace. Going dark now."

I muted my mike and started up the ladder, trying to keep quiet. I doubted that anyone in the engineering room would be able to hear me from this distance, but it was best to be careful. I went up the ladder rung by careful rung, then slowly stuck my head into the crawlway.

That saved my life.

The maintenance crawlway was a narrow tunnel about four feet in diameter, the walls and ceiling lined with pipes and bundles of wires. The first thing I saw was the sleek black shape of a security drone just to the right of the ladder cylinder, clinging to the ceiling overhead. The gun turret on the metal spider's back started to turn, the barrel of its weapon swinging towards me.

I reacted on pure instinct. I couldn't get my gun up in time to fire, so I didn't even try. Instead I pulled myself up the ladder, slamming into the wall, and the barrel of the turret gun whacked across my chest.

That hurt. A lot.

If someone has ever hit you with a length of steel pipe, it felt exactly like that. Pain just exploded through my chest, and I was pretty sure that I had cracked or broken a rib. I was mashed between the wall and the barrel of the drone's gun, but that meant the drone couldn't bring its weapon to bear. For a moment the barrel pushed hard against me, squeezing the breath from my chest as I fumbled with my machine pistol.

The drone's AI realized that it would have to move to shoot me, so it skittered backwards along the ceiling, the turret on its back rotating. But the with barrel of the gun gone from my chest, I could lift my machine pistol.

I opened fire. The noise in the enclosed crawlway was immense. The bullets ripped down the side of the drone, punching through its metal shell and hammering into its guts before it managed to get any shots off. The drone shuddered and then went limp, falling from the ceiling with a clang. I put three more shots into it for good measure, but it didn't move.

The smell of gun smoke and charred electronics filled the crawlway.

I took a deep breath, which hurt a lot. Something was flashing and wondered if I had somehow gotten a concussion in the process, and then realized that someone was texting me. I pulled my comm off my belt and saw that Corbin had sent me message consisting of a single question mark. I replied awkwardly—KILED DRNE—and then crawled past the dead machine, making my way down the passage. My chest felt tight with pain, and crawling wasn't pleasant, but I managed it, forcing myself along.

The question. Did I dare continue, given that I had just alerted everyone in the engineering room below that someone was up here? I didn't really have much choice, I realized, considering that my uncle and the others were about to storm the room. I had to gamble that the men below would assume the noise had been the drone doing its job.

I took a deep breath, asked every deity whose name I could remember and the nameless spirit of hyperspace to help me out, if they were so inclined, and continued crawling.

Soon I was over the engineering room.

Every few yards along the crawlway were access hatches that opened in the engineering room, both for maintenance and emergency escape from in case of a chemical leak or a hull breach or something. I brought up my phone again, connected to the security subsystem, and accessed the engineering room camera. As before, the image was terrible, and even worse on my phone's little screen. Yet I could see that the commandos had set up an impromptu barricade by the doors, sheltering behind stacks of crates, and another group waited halfway across the room, ready to reinforce the men guarding the door. It was a reasonable defensive formation, and it meant the commandos were separated into two distinct groups.

So much for dropping a single grenade on their heads.

I crawled forward, counting off the distance in my head. I reached a point about halfway through the engineering room, and I switched my gun's safety back on and holstered it. I pulled out four stun grenades and set the timers on each grenade to four seconds. Then I checked to make sure that I could hold two grenades in one hand.

The timing was going to be everything.

I dug out my multitool and undid the release on the nearest hatch. I took a deep breath, gripped the handle, and pushed, sending the hatch swinging downward on its hinges. It swung in silence, thank God. About eight meters below me I saw the engineering room, lights flashing on the various system consoles. There were quite a lot of red lights. The system was evidently not happy that Corbin had taken the regulator's CPU.

I could also see the commandos waiting for Corbin's attack. Fortunately, none of them had looked up just yet. Any minute one of them would happen to notice the opened hatch in the ceiling, and I had to be moving by then. I multitool into my belt and took a deep breath to calm myself, which was probably a bad idea because it sent a wave of pain through me.

Now or never.

I withdrew, seized two grenades in each hand, leaned over the edge of the hatch, and threw them. The grenades in my left hand I threw towards the commandos guarding the door. The grenades in my right hand I flung towards the men waiting in reserve.

The movement caught one man's attention, and he looked up and shouted a warning, his Tanith-Mordecai K7 snapping towards me.

I threw myself backwards just as a volley of automatic fire ripped up through the hatch. The bullets missed me and tore into the ceiling, bits of insulation from the pipes and the wiring falling onto the grillwork. The floor shivered beneath me as the bullets struck the metal, and rows of sharp bumps appeared all around me. The metal was strong enough to cause the rounds to fragment, but only just, and if one of the commandos had the bright idea of firing a laser at me, I was finished.

Then the stun grenades went off.

A brilliant flash of light blazed through the opened hatch, and even from this height I felt the vibration shoot through the metal. Then the shooting began in earnest, accompanied by the sounds of men screaming in rage and terror and agony. I crawled back towards the opened hatch and peered into the engineering room. It was all smoke and chaos, with the muzzle flashes of weapons visible in the gloom, and there was enough smoke that I could see the beams of the burst laser pistols.

A commando ducked for cover behind the console dedicated to managing the ion thrusters. It gave him excellent cover from the doors, but terrible cover from my position, so I lined up my pistol, sighted along the end, and pulled the trigger. Even with my sub-standard gun skills, I hit him in the helmet, and his head jerked before he slumped to the ground. Another commando noticed, looked up, and started to take aim at me, but before he pulled the trigger, a burst laser shot hit him in the chest and he spun.

I moved back and took cover, since I couldn't see through the increasingly heavy smoke and I couldn't see any likely targets.

But after another two or three exchanges of roaring gunfire, the engineering room fell silent. I peered over the edge again, trying to see what was happening.

"XO, this is Rovio," said Corbin's voice in my ear. "Engineering secure. I repeat, the engineering room is secure. Everyone, check in. We've got some men down."

"Nikolai here," I said, tapping my earpiece. "I'm all right." I shut the hatch, crawled over it, and made my way to the access ladder. I heard Nelson check in, followed by the other men. Four of the men didn't check in, which meant they were dead or too wounded to speak.

I reached the ladder and clambered down to the engineering room. The room smelled of gun smoke, burned armor, and blood, and the black-armored commandos lay sprawled over the ground. Nelson and two of the techs were moving over the dead men, methodically stripping them of guns and grenades. I spotted Corbin standing near the console that controlled the hypermatter reactor.

"Any word on what they were doing down here?" said Hawkins.

"Looks like they were getting ready to eject the hypermatter reactor," said Corbin, scrolling through lines of text on one of the displays.

"Did you get Ducarti?" said Hawkins. "Or the captain?"

"Nelson's still looking," said Corbin, "but I don't think either of them were down here."

I stopped by the console, and Corbin looked up, smiling.

"Nikolai," he said. "Good work. They were well and truly stunned when we stormed the room. They put up a fight, but less than I expected."

"Yeah," I said, looking at one of our own fatalities. He lay near a set of storage lockers that held vacuum suits for hull repairs. I hadn't known him well, but we had worked together on a dozen repair jobs, and now he was dead. "Well, at least we're not all dead… yet."

Corbin nodded, glancing back at the display. "You all right?"

"Didn't get shot," I said. "I might have broken a rib drone-wrestling. Suppose I had better wait to visit the infirmary until the men who got shot have been treated."

"Afraid so," said Corbin. "Did you see where Ducarti and the captain went?"

"I didn't see them at all," I said. "Maybe they went to the crew decks."

"XO?" said Corbin. "What's going on up there?"

For a moment there was silence, and then my earpiece crackled again.

"The commandos just surrendered," said Hawkins, and I let out a long sigh of relief. "Looks like they realized the writing was on the wall. The chief engineer wound up down there, and he's taking charge. We should have the commandos secured and the crew back to their stations within the hour. I think we've managed to successfully take back the *Rusalka*, Rovio."

"Do you have Ducarti or the captain?"

"No sign of them."

"They're not here either."

"Then where are they?" said Corbin, his voice sounding strained. "Rodriguez, Murdock. You there?"

"We are," said Murdock, his rough voice cutting into the channel. "Rodriguez is bringing full life support back. I've got most of the systems back on line. Still working on weaps. Got shields, though."

"Good, they can't hole us if they're on *Vanguard* now," said Corbin. "Get on the internal sensors, Rodriguez. Find Ducarti and the captain. They have to be somewhere and they're probably heading for the airlock to the troopship."

"Maybe they're going to steal a cargo drone," I said. Corbin squinted at me, puzzled. "Both the troopship and the *Vanguard* are docked along the *Rusalka's* dorsal corridor, right? If they're going to make a run for it, they can't use the dorsal corridor because we'd shoot them dead. So maybe they'll take over a cargo drone and ride it to their ship."

"I doubt it, neither of them are technical," said Murdock. "Here, Rodriguez. I'll get on the other console. You take the infrareds, I'll use the weapons detectors."

I listened with half of an ear as they talked, my eyes returning to the dead crewman on the floor near me.

The dead crewman, and the open lockers behind him.

The lockers that should have been closed. The lockers that should have been holding pressure suits.

The empty lockers.

"Uh oh," I said.

My uncle frowned.

"I think I know where Ducarti and Williams went," I told him.

Chapter 9
EVA For Beginners

"I should have thought of it sooner," said Corbin, slapping his palm against the console.

We had gathered around the master console in the engineering room, since it had the biggest displays. Arthur patched in several views from the external cameras, and the main display showed a good view of the *Rusalka's* exterior, the big freighter's running lights throwing the cylindrical hull into stark relief. It meant we had an excellent view of the two vacuum-suited figures making their way across the hull towards the closer of the two ships attached to it, the *Vanguard*. One of the figures moved with the easy grace of long zero-G experience, while the other lumbered along with clumsy steps.

Williams and Ducarti.

"A distraction," said Nelson, shaking his head with contempt. "That's all this was. He sacrificed all ten of his men in here and the five on the crew deck to cover his escape, the coward."

"Trust me, Chief," I said. "That's his style."

"It's over, then," said Hawkins. "He gets into the *Vanguard* and escapes, and that's that."

"No, it's not," said Corbin. "Our reactors are still entangled. I've got the hypermatter regulator back online, but it will be another four or five hours before the reactor is stable enough for a proper reboot. Ducarti has decided to cut his losses. He'll go for the troopship. He can wait in-system for a week for the Party rescue ship to pick him up after we blow."

"Then why are they headed for the *Vanguard*?"

"Probably to prevent our access to it," my uncle had a grim expression on his face as he answered the XO. "Ducarti won't want to let us board it and either disentangle the regulators or use its weapons to take out the troopship before he can get clear."

"And we'll all be dead," said Murdock over the phone.

"Not if I can help it," said Corbin. "Any chance of getting any weapons online?"

"None," said Murdock. "Williams left them locked, and there are no backdoors that I know about. It wouldn't matter until he uncoupled anyway. It's not as if any of our guns can target anything on the hull."

"A cargo drone," I said.

They all looked at me.

"What about my drones?" said Arthur with alarm.

"They can maneuver in zero-G. So we send one to ram the troopship."

"That's crazy," said Murdock. "It has combat-grade hull armor. Those cargo drones are flimsy little boxes with antigrav units, ion thrusters, and a bunch of manipulator arms. Hitting the ship with a drone won't do more than put a dent in it."

"No," I said, "what if we hitched a ride with the drone?"

They all looked at me again.

"Are you seriously suggesting," said Nelson, "that the drone carries us out to catch Ducarti?"

"Why not?" I said. "We've got suits. We can't catch up with them spacewalking, but we can ride."

"Not anymore," said one of the other techs. "It looks like Williams destroyed all the spacesuits when he left."

"What about the EVA packs?" I said.

The techs stared at each other.

"Those are still intact," said the tech.

"The three of us have still got our suits," I said, pointing at Corbin and Nelson.

"These suits aren't rated for EVA in hard vacuum," said Nelson.

"Not for working outside," said Corbin, his voice thoughtful. "But they're rated for two hours. That's long enough." He frowned at me. "You up for this?"

"No," I said. "I want to go lie down with a bottle of painkillers. But Ducarti's going to blow up the ship and kill us all. If we're going to catch him, this is our one shot."

My uncle nodded and looked at the chief.

"Kid's right," said Nelson with a sigh. "If we're going to go, we've got to go now."

Hawkins said several words that the Officers' Manual of Starways Hauling Company stated that officers were never to use under any circumstances. Then he held up his hand. "All right. God go with you, Rovio, Nelson, Nikolai."

"Good luck," said Murdock.

"We'll need it," said Corbin. "Rodriguez, fire up a cargo drone and send it to the engineering room airlock. Nelson, Nikolai, let's get ready."

We hastily checked our suits, donning our helmets and gauntlets once more. One of the techs wrestled out the EVA packs and we pulled them on. The heavy packs had gas thrusters, allowing movement and maneuverability outside of the ship in zero-G. Ducarti and Williams had taken a pair of the packs, so I wondered why they hadn't just flown straight to the *Vanguard*.

"You ever used one of these before?" said Nelson, passing me a fully loaded K7 rifle. I attached it to my suit's magnetic harness.

"Yeah," I said. "Once."

That was why they hadn't tried to fly. EVA packs were tricky to handle. Ducarti could barely handle walking on the hull.

Nelson sighed again. "Well, it beats sitting around waiting to explode, anyhow."

"I'm sending the number three drone." Arthur's voice came over my helmet's speakers. "Better get ready."

"We're ready," said Corbin. "Come on!"

The chief and I followed him through the engineering room and into the airlock. The room had one airlock, designed to allow the crewers to escape in the event of a disaster that cut off the dorsal corridor. It passed closer to the sublight drive plumes than I would have liked, but we ought to be safe from the drive radiation.

Of course, if we couldn't stop the two Socials, it didn't really matter.

The airlock cycled, and the outer door swung open, revealing the vacuum of space, a thousand times a thousand stars blazing in all directions. As we stepped free of the ship's artificial gravitics, I activated the magnetic gripping system in my boots, and followed Nelson and Corbin as they clambered onto the *Rusalka's* outer hull. My inner ear wasn't at all happy, which combined with my headache and the unending pain in my chest made for an unpleasant sensation. Spinning off the hull would have been even more unpleasant, though, so I clomped onwards, following the older men.

Walking atop the ship's outer hull was a weird feeling. With the gentle curvature and the various protrusions of thruster vents, sensor arrays, shield generators, and docking ports, it was like walking through a really strange skateboard park. I saw the hump of the dorsal corridor running along the ship's spine, and in the distance, the sleek, predatory mass of the *Vanguard* hovering over the ship like a hawk about to feast upon its prey. The *Vanguard* couldn't have gotten any closer to the *Rusalka* without ripping off part of its hull, so an airlock tube extended from the ship's nose to the side of the dorsal corridor.

That would be Ducarti's target. All he'd have to do was sever the airlock connection to decouple the two ships and the *Vanguard* would float off into space until the tangled reactors went critical. And there would be nothing we could do to stop it; ejecting the reactor from *Rusalka* couldn't be done outside of a shipyard.

I couldn't see either Ducarti or Williams yet, but I knew they were somewhere out there ahead of us.

"We're ready," came Murdock's voice over my helmet's speakers.

"Here comes the drone," said Arthur.

Blue light flashed as the dark bulk of the cargo drone moved overhead, swooping in low towards the hull. Unlike the drone that Arthur had used to defend himself, this drone was still intact, and it looked like a combination of a praying mantis and a big metal jellyfish. The drone slowed, its ion thruster flaring, and came to a stop a few meters from the hull. Of course, neither the *Rusalka* nor the drone had come to a complete stop, but were following identical velocities and vectors so they merely appeared to be at a stop relative to each other, but my head hurt too much to do the necessary math just now.

"Nice flying," said Murdock's voice.

"Thank you," said Arthur.

It was nice to hear them getting along, but my uncle was unimpressed.

"Rodriguez, how are we getting onto that thing?"

"The container manipulator arm," said Arthur. One of the drone's arms extended, stopping maybe a half-meter from the hull. It was a big three-pronged thing, designed to grip onto the top of heavy shipping containers. "I will lock it in place, and the drone will ferry you over to the *Vanguard*."

"How far are Ducarti and the captain from it?" said Nelson.

"About ninety meters," said Hawkins. "Get on your ride, gentlemen!"

"Let's go," said Corbin. His armored hand reached for the control arm of his EVA pack. "Short burst, and then we'll head for the *Vanguard*. Go!"

I squeezed my own control arm, using the weakest possible thrust setting. The EVA pack gave me a gentle kick, and I drifted off the hull and into the manipulator arm. Even that hurt a lot, and I barely managed to grab one of the prongs of the manipulator arm.

Turns out that using an EVA pack with a cracked rib isn't any fun.

"It is possible," I said to myself, "that I might be an idiot."

I'd forgotten my radio was still on.

"Once you get to a certain age, son," said Nelson, "you feel like that most of the time."

"Not me," said Murdock.

"Rodriguez, we're on board," said Corbin with a hint of asperity. I wondered if he had put up with this level of backtalk while in the Coalition navy. "Get us to the *Vanguard*. Murdock, can you target the captain and Ducarti on our HUDs?"

"Roger," said Murdock. The HUD in my helmet flickered, and in the distance I saw a faint red blotch. The HUDs in these suits were pretty basic, mostly devoted to oxygen levels, but they could display the locations of our two enemies.

It looked like Ducarti and Williams were almost underneath the *Vanguard*. If we were lucky, they'd only be armed with laser cutters and it would take them a few minutes to sever the reinforced metal of the airlock. At the speed the drone could move, we'd have plenty of time to stop them in the act.

Then the manipulator arm shuddered, and the drone started forward. I had half-feared that Arthur would accelerate so sharply that we'd be crushed in our unarmored suits, but he knew his business. The drone eased forward, the *Vanguard* growing larger and larger before us, the *Rusalka's* hull scrolling away to the left. The little red blotches representing Ducarti and Williams kept moving closer to the base of the airlock tube.

"Get ready to shoot," said Corbin. "Make it count."

Nelson raised his K7, and I lifted my rifle from its magnetic harness. It was clumsy in the suit gauntlets, but I managed. I wasn't at all sure of my ability to hit anything at this range, but Corbin and Nelson were better shots. We didn't have to be that accurate. We just had to pierce their suits in a few places, and Ducarti and Williams would die of asphyxiation.

Then there was an intense flash, bright enough against the deep black of space to cause my helmet filter to darken instantly. The bright reds and greens that impressed themselves into my closed eyes suggested it was a chemical reaction.

Which was to say, a shaped charge, or in more casual terms, a bomb.

"They blew the lock!" Hawkins shouted unnecessarily. The force of the silent explosion not only severed the connection between the *Vanguard* and the *Rusalka*, but also served to throw the smaller ship away from the much larger one. The warship's nose had been thrown back, so that it looked as if it was dismounting from *Rusalka* in a back handspring. It slowly tumbled away from the silver expanse of the hull in a somersault that would not stop until the ship exploded.

Now that the *Vanguard* was gone, we could see the troopship another 400 meters ahead. But we didn't see Williams or Ducarti.

"Where'd they go?" I asked.

"Maybe they blew themselves up," Nelson suggested optimistically.

"No, they're still there," Hawkins said. "They're right there!"

They must have lain flat against the hull to avoid having their suits punctured by debris from the bomb, but now they had gotten back on their feet and we could see them easily, right out in the open and exposed to our fire. But we were just as exposed to them.

"Now?" said Nelson.

Hawkins's voice crackled in my ears.

"Rovio!" he snapped. "Watch out! It looks like they're turning to shoot at you! Ducarti has some kind of launcher."

I couldn't hear anything, but a vibration went through the cargo manipulator arm. Williams was shooting and at least one of his shots had hit the drone. We knew the big machine could shrug off the hits, but K7 projectiles would tear through our suits like tissue paper.

"Now!" said Corbin. "Fire!"

Nelson snapped up his rifle faster than I would have thought possible and started shooting on full auto. Corbin followed suit, his boots locking to the metal of the arm, and I raised my gun and squeezed the trigger. We were shooting in almost total silence, which made the whole thing feel unreal.

Firing a vacuum-capable gun on full auto in zero-G is different than shooting one in a gravitized atmosphere. In gravity, the gun had both mass and weight, which helped keep it in your hands while firing. In zero-G, it had no weight, which meant it was harder to hold, and the kinetic motion of the K7 would send me shooting backwards like a booster rocket. Bracing the stock against my shoulder hurt, but I was ready for it, and my boots kept me from shooting off into the eternal void. Still, it spoiled my aim, and I doubt my shots went anywhere near Ducarti and Williams. I would have been surprised if they had come anywhere near the *Rusalka*, and the ship was a kilometer long.

At least I didn't shoot the chief or my uncle in the back.

They didn't have any better luck. The guns made no noise in the vacuum, and so I heard Hawkins without any trouble.

"You're overshooting!" said Hawkins. "Just a few meters off, shorten your aim. Wait! Get off the drone. Get off the drone! Incoming!!"

There was a second, smaller chemical flare from their position. This time my faceshield didn't darken.

"Take cover!" shouted Hawkins.

Where? We were standing on a cargo arm in vacuum. There wasn't anywhere to take cover.

"Eject!" said Corbin, and he leaped gracefully from the arm, the jets on his EVA pack shooting out white plumes. Nelson followed him, but I wasn't as practiced with using the EVA equipment.

I had just managed to shift my K7 to my right hand and grip the control arm with my left when the missile slammed into one of the drone's ion jets.

I couldn't hear the explosion, but I felt it, the vibration shooting through my boots and making my bones vibrate. The drone heaved to the side, spinning like a top, and it spun with enough force that the side of my head slammed into the drone's cargo arm. I heard a crunching noise, a squeal of static, and then I sort of went away for a while.

When I came to, I was spinning through nothingness, red and green lights flashing across my HUD.

Confusion filled my head, and then a jolt of sheer terrified panic pushed it aside. Ducarti's missile, the drone… I had been thrown off into space. I had a horrified instant when I thought I had fallen into a gravity well, that I would be pulled down into one of the gas giants' atmospheres to be cooked alive by their radiation, but then I remembered we were still hundreds of millions of kilometers from any of NR8965's planets, and at my current velocity, I would likely have a few billion years before my mummified corpse met that fate.

Well. That was that. I wouldn't die in a hyper-nuclear reaction, I just had to wait two or three hours until my suit failed in the hard vacuum. It could be worse. A better suit would just permit me to die a long and painful death of dehydration.

The nausea gripped me after that. I was still spinning around from the missile explosion, and my inner ear was not happy. My stomach heaved, and I was grateful there hadn't been time to eat anything during this awful day. Of all the ways to die, choking on my own vomit in a spacesuit would be one of the worst. Still better than getting cooked by drive radiation, though.

I groped for the control arm, firing the jets in the pattern I had practiced when studying for my certification tests. At last I got my spin under control, and I came to a halt relative to the ship's velocity. The gray cylinder of the *Rusalka* hovered ahead of me, glinting in its running lights, and I didn't think I was more than a thousand meters from the gargantuan ship.

"Corbin?" I said. "Anyone? Is anybody there?"

Only static answered me. I wondered if Ducarti had somehow managed to kill everyone on the ship when I was out, and then I noticed the red text on my HUD. My suit's life support system was still running, but the radio was dead. It had likely been damaged when my head bounced off the cargo arm. I The drone floated a few hundred meters away, still spinning ponderously away from the *Rusalka*, and I wondered if Corbin and Nelson were still alive, and if they had found a way to stop Ducarti. I looked towards where the troopship was above the *Rusalka*.

The airlock tube was gone. The ship had retracted it.

Even as I watched, harsh light flared around the cylindrical ship's drive nozzles as its sublight drive started to fire up. Ducarti and Williams were obviously safe and inside it. All they had to do now was fly sublight to a safe distance away from the doomed *Rusalka* and wait. With the weapons locked and the reactor-tangled *Vanguard* out of reach, there was nothing the XO, my uncle, or anyone on the crew could do.

Game over, man.

I should have been terrified. I ought to have been terrified. I think some part of me was terrified, knowing that I probably wouldn't even live long enough to die with the ship. I was aware of all that.

But, for some reason, I was mostly just pissed off.

Ducarti had murdered my mother and my brother. He had killed and maimed thousands of people on New Chicago, and he had gotten away scot-free, leaving behind nothing but a gloating message praising the cruel glories of the Revolution. He had gotten every single one of the men under his command killed, sacrificing their lives to save his own worthless hide. Now he would destroy the *Rusalka*, killing over a hundred men with whom I had worked over the last year, and once the Social Party rescue ship came to pick him up, he would get away scot-free again, and go on to ruin more lives and murder more innocent people.

The thought was intolerable. It was utterly and totally intolerable. And the only thing that could make my death worthwhile was if Ducarti died too. But how to manage that? The troopship wasn't a speed demon, but there was no way my little EVA jets could catch up with it. And even if they could, the accelerated mass of my body wouldn't so much as dent the troopship's heavy armor.

But the *Vanguard's* would do a lot more than dent it. And at her slow rate of relative movement, she couldn't have gone too far, somersaulting through the void. I wasn't trained on weapon systems, and I'd be more likely to crash her into the *Rusalka* than successfully dock her, but how hard could it be to smash her into the troopship? Being built to survive battle, the warship was not only faster, she was also better armored than her sublight companion.

So where was she? I slowly turned myself around, looking for a black ship against the black background of space. But I knew what to look for, and before long I noticed a starless patch of space that appeared to be moving. Then there was a flash, which I realized must be the exposed metal of the ruptured airlock, and I knew it had to be her.

I jammed the control arm forward, throwing the EVA jets to full power, and shot towards what I was pretty sure was the *Vanguard*. The motion made my injured ribs and head ache with further pain, but I was too angry to care. Sure enough, as I came closer I could see that it was indeed the slowly rotating ship that had been blocking out the stars. The sleek black shape loomed closer, and I aimed for the ship's underside, heading for the cargo airlock there.

I curved around the underside of the *Vanguard*, firing the EVA jets to slow my approach, and the cargo airlock came into sight. I hit the dark metal of the hull and scrabbled at the airlock's control. It was locked, but I pulled the panel off, and within I saw that the lock's mechanism was a simple one. The red wire went there, the green wire went there, and… the outer door slid open!

I threw myself into the airlock, knowing that an alarm would be going off on the ship's bridge. I slammed on the cycle control, activated my magnetic boots, and hit the override. The inner door slid open, and a gale of wind slammed into me with enough force to throw me into the void. I was ready for it, though, and I seized the frame of the inner door, pulling myself forward one agonizing step at a time. I flipped over the airlock, grabbing at the wall, and the inner and outer doors slammed shut behind me.

Right. So, I was on board the *Vanguard*. Now what?

The bridge. I had to get to the bridge. Maybe I would get lucky, and find that Ducarti had left the weapons systems unlocked. I hurried forward. I lost my K7 in the explosion, but the machine pistol still rode in my belt, and I drew the weapon, flipping off the safety. I also still had half a dozen stun grenades and two fragmentation ones. I didn't think anyone was still on the *Vanguard*, but we might have miscounted, and Ducarti could have left another security drone or two lying around.

The corridor ended in a ladder, and I climbed up, peering over the edge before hauling myself over the top rung. The ladder ended in a room that looked like a combined galley and crew lounge, with a pair of tables bolted to the floor and a pair of darkened screens on the wall. I had never been on a ship like this before, but it was atmosphere capable, which meant the bridge would be towards the nose.

I ran up the next corridor, went through a door, and found myself on the bridge. It was an oval room lined with consoles, with several free-standing stations arranged around the perimeter. The systems looked different, and much more expensive, than those on *Rusalka*, but the basic principles were the same.

I hurried over to the tactical console and tried it. No good. Ducarti had left the ship's weapons locked. If I had been lucky, I could have blasted his troopship to dust, but that would have been too easy.

It didn't matter. He wasn't getting away, not this time.

Think. I had to think. My head felt like it was full of cotton and broken glass. I couldn't let Ducarti get away, but I had to try and save the others. The hypermatter reactors were still entangled. Corbin would have started stabilizing the *Rusalka's* reactor by now, but it had to be synced from here.

I pushed away from the tactical console and dropped into the pilot's chair.

And then, to my relief, I saw that Ducarti had not locked the navigation and engine controls. I set about figuring out the controls, trying to concentrate through the growing pain. The first thing I did was fire up the comms. I hailed *Rusalka* as I brought up the reactor controls, and someone answered after a few moments.

"This is the *Rusalka*," said Hawkins, sounding suspicious.

"XO, it's Nikolai," I said. "I'm on the *Vanguard*."

"What?" said Hawkins. "How? We lost track of you after the explosion. Rodriguez sent one of his drones to pick up Corbin and Nelson, but–"

"Sir," I cut him off, "I can shut down the hypermatter reactor from here."

He was silent for a moment as the significance of that caught up to him.

"Right," he said. "The regulator is working again. Our reactor is stable enough that we should be able to do it too. So long as we do it in sync, it should work. Murdock!"

Murdock's rough voice came into the channel. "You there, Rovio?"

"Yeah," I said. "I'm ready to shut down."

I heard him shouting at someone, probably Arthur. "All right. Tell the reactor to shut down at this timestamp." A number flashed on the console. "You got that?"

"Underway," I said. I entered the commands, the reactor diagram on the console flashing green and yellow. "Doing it in three… two… one… now."

I keyed the reactor for shutdown, and braced myself, half-expecting the ship to blow up beneath me.

But the ship didn't explode. For a moment the console display remained the same, and then it flashed blue. The reactor had shut down.

I heard cheering in the background.

"Rovio, it worked," said Hawkins. "Our reactor is shut down. Yours?"

"Offline," I said. "It worked, too."

Then I reached over and shut off the comm channel.

I was pretty sure Hawkins wouldn't approve of what I was about to do.

Ducarti wasn't getting away. Not this time. I wasn't a pilot, but I knew the basics, and more to the point I knew how to operate the macros. I brought up a local sensor display, and saw the troopship heading towards one of the gas giants. Ducarti probably thought it would be safe to hide there until someone came to pick him up, or perhaps he had supplies stashed there.

I locked the navigation computer onto the troopship and fired up the sublight engines. The gravitics kept the acceleration from ripping me apart, but I still felt the shudder go through the ship. The sensor displays shifted as the *Vanguard* rapidly began to gain on the troopship. The troopship had a good start, but the blockade runner had far more powerful engines, and it soon began to close on the troopship.

The *Vanguard* also had substantially better armor. I was counting on that.

The comm flashed again, and I accepted the call.

This time the video display lit up, showing the bare metal interior of a troopship's control deck. Ducarti was in the pilot's chair, Williams was sitting next to him, looking more like a scared child than a spaceship captain.

"Rovio," spat Ducarti. "I should have known that… wait. No. Not the elder. The younger! Nikolai! You are becoming very nearly as problematic as your uncle."

"Thanks," I said. "It's over, Ducarti. You lost. You can drop the act now. Any last words?"

"Hardly," said Ducarti, his eyes narrowing. "I presume you have stabilized the reactors. But while you may control both ships now, you don't have control of either vessel's weapons, or someone would have fired by now. So. Chase us around the system if you wish. It will be an entertaining diversion until my rescue ship arrives and blasts you both out of the sky."

"It would be," I said. "Except your ship isn't all that fast. You can outrun the *Rusalka*, but you can't outrun me."

"So?" said Ducarti, still smiling. "It is not as if you will be able to board us. You…"

His voice trailed off. Williams's eyes widened in stark terror.

I ignored him. I was watching Ducarti's face.

I smiled as he got it.

And at last that smug expression vanished.

He snarled a course and started punching commands into the control board, taking evasive action. It didn't make any difference. The *Vanguard's* thrust-to-mass ratio was far superior, and the blockade runner continued to close. Ducarti snarled, and then his eyes widened. He started entering a new series of commands, one after another.

My control board lit up. He was trying to take remote control of the ship, logging into it from the troopship. I couldn't do anything about that. The tactical console was locked, and so were the main computer functions. He had left the engines and maneuvering accessible, but once he logged into the computer, he could take control of the ship. His most likely move would be to shut off life support and let me asphyxiate.

But I was ready for that. The system would not let me access the more critical system functions, but I could run all the non-critical applications I wanted. I still had Arthur's drive with me, so as Ducarti logged in, I plugged the drive into the console, and told the computer to run the harmless program on it, devoting every available processing cycle to it.

Every screen except for the comm display went black.

"What?" said Ducarti.

Then the displays lit up again, and every single screen showed the main menu for *Gunno-Tatakai*. The terrible music blasted from the speakers, so loud it made my teeth vibrated, and for an instant Ducarti looked bewildered.

"What is that noise?" he demanded.

"Music," I said. "If you can call it that."

He snarled again and kept frantically tapping screens.

I couldn't keep him from logging in. He had root-level access to the ship's computer. But with *Gunno-Tatakai* hogging every bit of system resources it could access, the system was sluggish and slow to respond. At last Ducarti seized control of the ship, crashed the game process, and shut off the engines.

It was too late. I tapped the controls to buckle me in, then watched the numbers measuring the gap drop between the two ships drop to three digits, then two.

The *Vanguard* rammed into the troopship, the armored blockade runner ripping through the troopship like a hammer through a wooden box. The comm channel remained open for a split second after that, and I heard Ducarti scream, saw fire start to bloom through the control deck.

The image and sound dissolved into static.

The *Vanguard* was armored, but the ship still shuddered and screamed from the tremendous impact.

Eventually the shaking stopped, and I hauled myself back into the pilot's seat as the lights went out on the bridge. The ship's computer was still carrying out Ducarti's final commands. I finally managed to get the comm system restarted on the third try.

"Rovio?" Hawkins answered my call. "Are you all right? What happened out there?"

"Hey, XO," I said, pulling off my helmet and letting it drop to the floor. "Actually, I suppose you're captain now. Or acting captain." My head hurt and seemed to be expanding and contracting in time with my heartbeat. "Okay, so, situation update. I ran right up his exhaust so he couldn't get away."

"You're saying," said Hawkins, incredulous, "that you flew *Vanguard* right into Ducarti's ship?"

"Rammed is the preferred term," I said. "Historically sound naval tactic. Say, you should probably send someone to help me out. I think I have a concussion, maybe some broken ribs."

"I'll have your uncle put together a boarding party," said Hawkins. "He and Nelson made it back to the ship okay."

"Oh, good," I said. "A party! Like with presents and cake?"

"Rovio," said Hawkins, sounding concerned. "Are you okay?"

"Sure," I said. Then, apparently, I passed out.

Victory is supposed to feel glorious, but I didn't feel anything at all.

Chapter 10

The Law of Salvage

I don't remember the next couple of days very well.

Turns out I was hurt worse than I thought.

I did indeed have a concussion, which wasn't a surprise, and two cracked ribs, which was fewer than I would have guessed. I also suffered some moderate hearing loss from the explosion, and sprains in both ankles from getting blasted off the drone. I had also lost a lot of blood—the bullet that clipped my shoulder had made a mess, and I didn't think there was an inch of my body that didn't have a bruise or three.

So I got my own bed in the infirmary after all.

I can vaguely recall the medical drones rolling back and forth between the beds. They shot me up with a lot of drugs designed to stimulate bone growth, and deal with cranial trauma, and some really excellent painkillers. I think I slept for a couple of days, and when I finally woke up, I still felt terrible, but my head was mostly clear.

Given that I wasn't dead, that was a good thing.

Arthur visited me once I woke up.

"You actually killed them with *Gunno-Tatakai?*" he said, sounding awed.

"Never seen a computer system that game can't slow down," I said, sipping at my water.

We traded news. The *Rusalka* was in hyperspace again, with the damaged *Vanguard* safely clamped to the hull. The surviving commandos were secured in one of the cargo bays; Corbin planned to drop them off at the first habitable planet, then send Coalition intelligence to pick them up. He and the other techs had been working around the clock to repair the damage to the *Rusalka*, but there wasn't much left that we could do without a shipyard. The ship had come through the hijacking and the mutiny more or less intact, even though the computer would have to be wiped and the operating system reinstalled to unlock all the subsystems.

Arthur laughed. "I wish I could have seen the expression on the captain's face."

"It was like this." I opened my eyes and mouth as wide as I could. "Only more scared."

He laughed. For me, though, the helpless fury in Ducarti's eyes would be something I would take to my grave. Something satisfying.

We talked a bit more, and he left me some of his game collection, which was nice because I didn't have anything to do.

My uncle visited me later that day.

"How are you feeling?" he said.

"Everything hurts," I said, "but I'm not dead or crippled, so I shouldn't complain."

"That was absolutely insane! What were you thinking?" Corbin was still angry with me, but then he relented. "It could have been much, much worse. We all made mistakes."

"You couldn't have known the captain would have sided with Ducarti," I said.

"No," said Corbin. "But I should have. We should all have realized some things sooner. Ducarti made mistakes, too." He shook his head. "He probably should have shot you right away."

"I expect he wished he had," I said. "Just before he went the way of all atoms. Where are we going next?"

"Our next stop is a Coalition naval station," said Corbin. "We'll also have to file a complete mutiny, hijacking, and piracy report, which will be a lot of work. I expect the legal tangle will take a month or two to clear up."

"Well," I said, "I'm just glad I'm alive to see it. Considering the alternative, I'll take a few weeks of legal entanglements."

"Oh, don't worry," said my uncle. "I think you'll get more than that."

As it turned out, the legal mess took three months, not two.

Once we delivered New Sibersk's cargo of grain to the port on New Celadon, I was interviewed by what felt like every anti-piracy and intelligence officer in the Coalition navy. I had to describe the events over and over and over again, which was more than a little annoying, but then, it was on company time, so I got paid for it. I wasn't about to complain. I had been half-afraid there would be some sort of murder or manslaughter charges against me or the other crew members for killing the Socials, but the investigating authorities decided that it was a clear-cut case of self-defense, so we were all clear on that front.

As it turned out, there had been numerous bounties upon Ducarti's head, so many that the total came to a fairly large sum of money. I didn't really want it, since it felt like blood money, but fortunately the corporate policy of Starways required that the money be divided equally among the crew, so that was all right. The dead crew members got their share too, which was good since some of them left widows and orphans behind.

For a few weeks I was a minor celebrity. It turned out that a lot of people all over the Thousand Worlds had hated Ducarti almost as much as I did. Some small colony on the spiral side of the Thousand Worlds even gave me an official vote of thanks, since Ducarti had apparently set off some kind of virulent bioweapon on their world. For nearly a month, a gaggle of reporters followed me everywhere, but I always pushed them off on Hawkins, who had been promoted to captain of the *Rusalka*.

There was one thing, however, that I could not get rid of so easily.

"The *Vanguard*?" I said.

"It's yours," said Corbin.

We sat in a little coffee shop across the street from Starways Hauling Company's local office, following yet another lengthy meeting with the company's legal counsel. Almost everything had been dealt with—all the papers signed, all the testimony given, all the insurance paid and collected, and all the billion other little paperwork problems our misadventure with Ducarti had generated were approved, stamped, filed, sealed, and otherwise completed to the approval of the relevant bureaucracy.

"The Coalition's position is clear," said Corbin, "as are all the legal traditions of the major worlds. You captured a pirate ship. What's more, you did it single-handed."

"Is it still a capture when no one's aboard?" I said.

"Close enough," said Corbin, holding up one last bundle of papers. "Point is, the *Vanguard* legally qualified as a prize vessel, and it is now your ship."

I sat back, flabbergasted. My own ship! How amazing would that be? For a moment I had a wild fantasy of flitting around the Thousand Worlds as an independently wealthy trader and epic playboy.

Reality abruptly dashed my vision.

"I'll have to sell it," I said. "She's pretty banged up and I can't afford the repairs. How much do you think we could get for her."

"Actually," said Corbin, "I might know someone who would be willing to foot the bill to set her straight."

"You do?" I said. "Who?"

"Coalition Intelligence," said Corbin.

I didn't say anything for a while.

"We would have others buy shares in the ship, of course," said Corbin. "We'd make it affordable for Murdock and Nelson and a few of the others. Arthur Rodriguez too. They'd serve as a front corporation. Most of the funding would come from the agency."

"So what would we do with the ship, then?" I said. "It's kind of big to spy with."

"Make money, of course," said Corbin. "There is a lot of demand for ships of that class to move small cargoes. And as we travel around the Thousand Worlds, we can do little favors for Coalition intelligence and to upset the Social Party. It's a good fight, Nikolai. You know better than most the kind of harm the Social Party can do." He shrugged. "I won't pressure you either way. If you want to stay with Starways, God knows you'll rise high with all the recommendations from the *Rusalka's* crew. But I think this would be the best course."

I sat in silence for a moment. I had left New Chicago to get away from the destruction the Socials had wrought there, but it had followed me onto the *Rusalka* anyway. Ducarti had met his deserved fate, and I wondered how many more men like him were out there.

And if we happened to get rich in the process, well, I couldn't object to that. Besides, if the vids could be trusted, girls always liked spies and secret agents. So perhaps my vision might come true after all.

"We're going to need a new name for her," I said. "We're not Socials. What do you think of *Retief*?"

My uncle grinned, drew a line through the word *Vanguard*, and pushed the contract over to me.

CASTALIA HOUSE

SCIENCE FICTION
Mutiny in Space by Rod Walker
Alien Game by Rod Walker
Young Man's War by Rod Walker
Superluminary by John C. Wright
City Beyond Time by John C. Wright
Back From the Dead by Rolf Nelson

MILITARY SCIENCE FICTION
There Will Be War Volumes I and II ed. Jerry Pournelle
Starship Liberator by David VanDyke and B. V. Larson
Battleship Indomitable by David VanDyke and B. V. Larson
The Eden Plague by David VanDyke
Reaper's Run by David VanDyke
Skull's Shadows by David VanDyke

FANTASY
Summa Elvetica by Vox Day
A Throne of Bones by Vox Day
A Sea of Skulls by Vox Day
The Green Knight's Squire by John C. Wright
The Dark Avenger's Sidekick by John C. Wright
Awake in the Night by John C. Wright

FICTION
An Equation of Almost Infinite Complexity by J. Mulrooney
The Missionaries by Owen Stanley
The Promethean by Owen Stanley
Brings the Lightning by Peter Grant
Rocky Mountain Retribution by Peter Grant

NON-FICTION
SJWs Always Lie by Vox Day
SJWs Always Double Down by Vox Day
The LawDog Files by LawDog
The LawDog Files: African Adventures by LawDog
A History of Strategy by Martin van Creveld